Sharks

"You lied to me, Maria."

I can't breathe, she thought.

I can't breathe, and I can't move my arms.

"I just hate to be lied to," he said flatly, his face expressionless.

Maria suddenly realized he wasn't staring at her. His gaze was over her shoulder, past her in the rolling waters. She turned to see what had caught his eye.

Dark shapes. Skimming rapidly along the surface of the water.

Like submarines. Dark triangles moving silently toward them.

Buddy returned his eyes to hers.

She saw the smile form on his face. The strangest smile.

"Sharks," he said.

Other Point thrillers
by R.L. Stine you will enjoy:

BEACH HOUSE

R.L. Stine

SCHOLASTIC INC.
New York Toronto London Auckland Sydney

No part of this publication may be reproduced in whole or in part, or stored in a retrieval system, or transmitted in any form or by any means, electronic, mechanical, photocopying, recording, or otherwise, without written permission of the publisher. For information regarding permission, write to Scholastic Inc., 730 Broadway, New York, NY 10003.

ISBN 0-590-45386-6

24 23 22 21 20 19 18 17 16 15   0 1 2/0

Printed in the U.S.A.   01

First Scholastic printing, August 1992

PART ONE

Summer of 1956

1
A Call for Help

"Ooh, turn up the radio," Maria said. "I love this song!"

Lying on her back, Amy reached lazily across the beach blanket and turned the knob on the red plastic radio. "Sh-Boom Sh-Boom," poured out of the speaker.

"Sh-Boom Sh-Boom Sh-Boom."

"I love the words," Amy said, giggling. "Who sings this?"

"The Crewcuts," Maria said, eyes closed under her pink plastic sunglasses. "This was the first record I bought when I got my new 45-player." She opened her eyes and pulled herself up on her elbows. "Can't you make it any louder?"

Amy shook her head, her tight blonde curls catching the golden light of the afternoon sun. "The batteries are almost dead. They only last a few hours."

"Sh-Boom Sh-Boom. Yadadadadadada."

3

"It's so neat!" Maria gushed. "I've played it over and over. I played it so much, the needle wore out and the record turned white."

Amy squinted up at her friend. "My dad would never let me buy a rock-and-roll record," she said unhappily. She fiddled with the shoulder straps of her bathing suit. Amy was small, very thin, with a boyish figure, and the blue and white flower-patterned, one-piece suit was a bit big on her. "He says it's just noise."

"Sh-Boom Sh-Boom . . ."

They settled back on the beach blanket, soaking up the sun's warmth, listening to the rest of the song. In front of them, the green-blue ocean waves rolled onto the sand, gentle, lapping waves. Children squealed happily, running along the shore. A few swimmers were testing the waters, still winter-cold.

Maria could feel the sun on her shoulders. I should put on more lotion, she thought. But she was feeling lazy today. So lazy . . .

The song ended, and the bright-voiced disc jockey's patter blared from the box-shaped portable radio. "And now the Singing Rage, Miss Patti Page." "Moonlight in Vermont" started. Amy turned the volume down.

"A whole summer of this," Maria said dreamily, closing her eyes contentedly. "Not bad, huh?"

"I think I can take it," Amy replied.

"Just lying on the beach, swimming in the ocean,

messing around in town." Grinning, Maria adjusted her ponytail, tugging at the rubber band that held it. She had straight, silky black hair, which she almost always kept swept back in a ponytail, with bangs cut straight across her forehead, an inch above her dramatic brown eyes.

"Don't forget Ronnie," Amy said, reaching for the bottle of suntan lotion. "Ronnie's here at Dunehampton for the whole summer, too."

"Lucky you," Maria said coyly.

Amy and Ronnie had been going steady for nearly a year. Maria thought they were a funny couple. Ronnie was so tall and lanky, he practically had to stoop over to talk to little Amy. He called Amy "Mouse," a nickname she hated. But Maria had to admit that with her tight blonde curls, gray-blue eyes, and tiny button nose, short, skinny Amy really *did* resemble a mouse.

A very cute mouse.

Maria tried not to be jealous of Amy, but it was hard. Maria didn't have a boyfriend. In fact, even with her dark, dramatic looks and her fun, enthusiastic personality, she had never gone steady with anyone.

Oh, well, she thought wistfully, gazing past her friend, watching the wide, yellow beach fill with sunbathers, maybe things will change this summer.

She and her aunt had arrived in Dunehampton a week ago, and Maria had already met two boys who seemed interested in her.

First there was Buddy. She had met Buddy her first day on the beach. He just popped up in the sand beside her, as if out of nowhere. He seemed lost, so Maria had started talking to him.

They had hit it off immediately. Buddy was good-looking in a clean-cut sort of way, but shy and awkward. And sort of clumsy. He was intense, very serious, Maria realized. He didn't like to kid around the way most kids did. As a result, Ronnie and some of the other guys went out of their way to tease him, to try to get his goat.

But Maria found herself drawn to Buddy, despite his earnestness, his awkward shyness. Buddy was . . . different.

And then there was Stuart. Stuart was a friend of Ronnie's, although he didn't go to their school. Ronnie had introduced Stuart to Maria in town.

Stuart was Mr. Rock and Roll. Mr. Real Cool Cat. Stuart was a lot of fun. Always joking, always messing around. Always snapping his fingers to some tune no one else could hear. Always combing his heavily Brylcreemed hair, which came up in a tall wave in front and then was swept into a ducktail over his shirt collar in back.

He thought it made him look tough. Maria guessed he wanted to look like the juvenile delinquents in *Rebel Without a Cause* or something.

But Stuart could never really look tough. He was too cute. Too funny.

Silly sometimes, Maria decided. In many ways, the opposite of Buddy.

She thought of the other evening when a whole group of teenagers, summer people as well as townies, had gathered on the beach back in the low, grassy dunes. She wasn't sure how it had started. Maybe someone had urged Stuart on, put the idea in his head. But all of a sudden, he had jumped up, pretending to play the guitar, and began leaping around like Bill Haley & the Comets, singing "Shake, Rattle & Roll" at the top of his lungs.

Before long, a whole bunch of guys had joined in, all of them shouting out "Shake, Rattle & Roll" and dancing about like wild men. And the girls had formed a big circle, laughing and clapping their hands, and chanting, "Crazy, man, crazy! Crazy, man, crazy!" in time to their singing.

It was so much fun.

But Buddy had just stood there with his hands in the pockets of his shorts. Trying to keep a forced smile on his face, but looking as uncomfortable as ever.

Clapping and chanting, Maria had spotted him at the edge of the circle. He was attempting to clap along, but couldn't get the rhythm.

She felt sorry for him, in a way.

Poor, serious Buddy.

Buddy and Stuart. Stuart and Buddy.

Yes, it might be an interesting summer, Maria decided.

"Hey — look at that girl!" Amy cried, poking Maria in the side excitedly, interrupting her thoughts.

Maria followed Amy's gaze several blankets down and saw a girl with short, red hair standing on the beach in a two-piece bathing suit, carrying a large picnic basket.

"Get a load of that bathing suit!" Amy declared. "It's so tiny."

"It's one of those French ones, I think," Maria replied, staring hard as the girl set the basket down.

"Huh?"

"I think they're called *bikinis*," Maria said. "I saw some pictures of them in *Look* magazine."

"Well, maybe they wear them in France," Amy said, unable to take her eyes off the girl, who knew that she was causing a commotion and that her bathing suit was attracting a lot of staring eyes. "But they'll never catch on here."

Maria laughed.

"Well, you'd never catch *me* in one!" Amy insisted. "Look — her belly button is showing!"

"I think it's kind of neat," Maria said. She started to say something else, but stopped when she saw Ronnie and Stuart running toward them at full speed, dodging blankets and beach umbrellas as they ran.

"Hey — what's happening?" Maria cried.

Surprised, both girls jumped to their feet, adjusting their bathing suits.

"It — it's Buddy!" Ronnie cried.

Both boys pointed to the ocean.

Staring past them, Maria saw him.

Buddy was in the water, pretty far out, the waves rolling him about.

And he was screaming, Maria saw.

Screaming at the top of his lungs.

Screaming for help.

2
Humiliated

"Buddy!" Maria cried in alarm.

She started to run toward the water, but stopped as she realized that Stuart and Ronnie were laughing.

They were both dripping wet, their baggy swim trunks clinging to their legs. Wet sand stuck to their feet as they approached the bewildered girls.

"Ronnie — what's so funny?" Amy demanded.

In the ocean, Buddy rolled with the waves, only his head and shoulders visible in the sparkling blue-green waters, one hand waving frantically at them.

"We've got to help him!" Maria insisted. "Why did you run away and leave him there?"

Stuart's grin grew wider. He held up a pair of navy-blue swim trunks. "We depantsed him."

"Huh?"

Maria saw Buddy gesturing frantically now, waving with both hands, his head tossed back as he

10

shouted, his cries drowned out by the steady wash of the waves.

"We depantsed him," Stuart repeated, waving the trunks in the air like a flag, taunting Buddy with them.

"Look at him! He'll freeze his — " Ronnie started.

Maria interrupted by grabbing the trunks from Stuart's hand and slapping Ronnie with them. "How could you do that? It's not funny!"

Ronnie quickly grabbed the wet trunks back. "Sure, it is!" he declared, and burst out laughing.

The other three burst out laughing, too.

It *was* pretty funny.

Especially watching Buddy bobbing in the waves, calling frantically, waving to them, unable to come out or even come close to shore.

"He'll freeze!" Maria said, glancing at the swim trunks, which Ronnie had wrapped around Stuart's head like a turban, and starting to laugh all over again. "The ocean is still freezing cold!"

"So?" Stuart asked with a shrug.

"Buddy *hates* jokes like that," Maria said. "Why are you two always picking on him?"

"Because he's so weird," Stuart answered quickly.

"Because he's so square," Ronnie added.

"Yeah. He's so square, he's cubed!" Stuart added.

"Poor guy," Amy said quietly, gazing at the water.

"Where's the lifeguard?" Maria asked, searching

the beach, her eyes stopping at the empty lifeguard post to their left. "How can they let Buddy carry on like that without — "

"The lifeguards don't start for another week," Amy said.

"Come on, Stuart — " Maria made a grab for the trunks, but Stuart dodged away, giggling. "Give Buddy back his trunks."

"Come and make me," he said playfully, pulling the trunks off his head and waving them at her like a toreador in a bullfight.

"Come on, guys. We can't leave him in there. Remember — there were sharks spotted real close to the shore yesterday. And there could be *jellyfish* out there!" Amy cried heatedly.

That made the two boys collapse in laughter.

Maria made a diving grab for the trunks, but missed.

That started an enthusiastic keep-away game, with the trunks flying from Stuart to Ronnie, and the girls making valiant but unsuccessful attempts to get them away.

Buddy had stopped calling and waving and was floating quietly now, watching the game.

"Got 'em!" Laughing, Maria grabbed the trunks and began running to the water.

She was at the edge of the shore, water lapping over her ankles, when Stuart, running hard, tackled her from behind. As she toppled forward onto the sand, she flung the trunks toward the ocean with all her strength.

"Ooof." She hit the wet sand hard with Stuart's arms still around her waist. "Get off me!"

He rolled away, laughing. When Maria looked up, Buddy's trunks were floating just beyond where the waves were breaking, and Buddy was desperately making his way to them, half-running, half-swimming, his handsome features tightened in anger.

"Oh, no," Maria groaned as the trunks sank out of sight, disappearing into the green waters before Buddy could get to them.

He made a surface dive as a tall, frothy wave crashed over his head. All four of them watched eagerly, waiting for him to reappear. A few seconds later, he floated up behind the wave, shaking his head, sputtering — without the trunks.

Stuart clapped his hands, laughing gleefully. "I saw his buns!"

They all laughed, even Maria. Buddy did look ridiculous, floundering around out there. Even she had to admit it.

He shook a fist at them and dived under another wave, swimming hard now, searching for the drowned swim trunks.

Again, he came up without them.

"Bring me another pair!" he cried breathlessly, swimming as close to shore as he dared.

"Huh? Can't hear you!" Stuart pretended, cupping a hand over his ear.

"A towel!" Buddy shouted unhappily. "Just bring a towel — okay?"

"Can't hear you!" Stuart repeated.

Buddy shouted his request again.

"I guess he wants us to leave," Stuart said and, taking Maria's hand, started to pull her away from the shore.

"Hey — Stuart — whoa! We can't just leave him like that!" Maria protested.

"Want to bet?" was Stuart's reply.

And before Maria quite realized what was happening, the four of them were walking away, shoving each other playfully, talking and laughing, with Stuart doing a very funny impression of Buddy trying to get off the crowded beach without any swim trunks.

A while later, with blue shadows sliding over the beach as the sun lowered behind the dunes, Maria collected her things, shoving them into her straw beach bag.

Sea gulls patrolled the sand, searching for items left behind by sunbathers. Terns hopped comically in blue puddles near the shoreline. A few swimmers braved the cold of the late afternoon ocean. But the waves were taller now, and the air carried the chill of approaching evening. Most people, including Amy and Ronnie, had packed up and headed home.

What a crazy afternoon, Maria thought, smiling to herself. That Stuart is such a clown.

And as she thought his name, he appeared beside her, an orange and yellow striped beach robe over his bathing suit, a towel slung over his shoulder. "Maria, what are you smiling about?"

She shrugged. "Just smiling."

Grinning, he pulled the towel off his shoulder and snapped it at her, deliberately missing. "Listen . . . uh . . . Ronnie and Amy are going to the Dune-hampton drive-in tonight."

"What's playing?" Maria asked, only half-listening as she struggled to squeeze the folded-up beach blanket into her bag.

"*Creature from the Black Lagoon*," Stuart said. "Want to come, too? I mean, with me?"

"Yes," Maria answered quickly. But then her smiled faded. "Oh, no. I mean, I can't. I sort of made plans to do something with Buddy."

Lugging the heavy straw bag in both hands, she began heading for home, making her way along the low dunes at the back of the beach.

"Buddy?" Stuart laughed, snapping his towel at a clump of tall dune grass. "He's probably still in the ocean!"

They both laughed. Maria stopped first. "That was so mean."

"Yeah. I know," Stuart said, grinning. "Where's he live, anyway? Is he a townie?"

"I don't think so," Maria replied. "He's staying in that new beach house that's at the end of the beach."

She pointed to it. The house, a large, hulking redwood structure, stood at the edge of the shore, jutting out into the ocean on tall, wooden stilts.

"Huh? I heard there's something weird about

that house. I heard it's been empty ever since it was built," Stuart said, stopping beside her to gaze at it.

"Not anymore," Maria told him. "I've seen Buddy there."

"Stand him up tonight," Stuart urged, still staring into the distance at the dark beach house.

"Huh? Why?" Maria started walking again.

"Because he has cooties," Stuart joked.

"Very mature," she scolded.

"No. Really. Stand him up," Stuart pleaded, hurrying to stay up with her, their bare feet padding silently along the soft sand of the dunes. "He's so . . . weird."

"He's very sensitive," Maria said, feeling she had to defend Buddy.

"Sensitive? You mean he has no sense of humor," Stuart replied heatedly. "He's a sourpuss. When he tries to smile, he looks like Howdy Doody. You know. Like his smile is painted on." He did an impression of Buddy's smile.

Maria burst out laughing. It was a really good impression. Buddy *did* look like that TV puppet Howdy Doody when he smiled.

"He's no fun at all," Stuart added, the wooden smile still locked on his face.

"Yeah. Well . . ." Maria had to admit that Stuart was right about that. Buddy wasn't exactly a million laughs.

But laughing wasn't everything, she argued with herself.

There was more to life than practical jokes and acting silly all the time.

"I like him because he's different," she told Stuart. "He's very smart."

Stuart groaned, insulted. "Dump him, Maria. I think I can borrow my dad's Thunderbird tonight. We can go to the drive-in in style!"

"You have a Thunderbird?" Maria set down the heavy basket for a second and turned to him. "What color?"

"Pink."

"Really?"

"With gray leather seats. It's a convertible."

"A Thunderbird convertible? I've never *been* in a Thunderbird convertible!" Maria exclaimed.

"So you'll dump Buddy and come with me tonight?" Stuart asked eagerly.

"Okay," Maria agreed. "I'll just make up some excuse for Buddy tomorrow. He'll get over it."

"All *reet!*" Stuart exclaimed happily, snapping his towel in the air. "Pick you up at seven, Maria." And with a cry of "Later, alligator!" he went running back in the other direction toward his parents' cottage.

Maria hoisted up the straw beach bag and started back on her way. The house her parents rented every summer was along the narrow road that led away from the dunes, just a ten-minute walk from the beach.

As she walked, she stared straight ahead at the dark beach house at the beach's end, now covered in gray-blue shadow as evening descended. Leaning out to the water, perched on its four tall stilts, the house looked as if it could walk away, step right into the water.

Darkened in shadow, it looked like a large, low animal huddled on the shore.

Who had built it in such a strange, dangerous spot? Maria wondered. All by itself. Half in the water.

And why did it stand empty for so long?

A glint of sunlight reflected red off one of the house's windows. The window immediately went dark again.

It's as if the house just winked at me, Maria thought.

Then, shifting the weight of her bag, she turned onto the road and began to follow it home.

As she walked, she didn't see the dark figure crouching low, hidden behind the low dune.

She didn't see Buddy, a beach towel wrapped around his waist, pressed tightly against the dune, peering over the tall grass, watching her. Listening.

Listening.

He had heard everything she and Stuart had said.

And as she disappeared around a curve in the road, he remained there in the puddle of darkness at the back of the dune.

Trembling all over.

Trembling so hard, his teeth chattered.

Trembling not from the cold.

But from anger.

3
Worried About Sharks

"Did you have a good time with Stuart?" Amy asked.

Maria nodded, smiling coyly.

"The movie was really neat," Amy said.

"Our speaker wasn't working too well," Maria said. "We had to move the car to three different spots before we found a good one."

It was the following afternoon, a bright but overcast day, hazy with a fog moving in off the ocean. The two friends had decided to take a long walk along the shore since the sun wasn't cooperating.

"Did Stuart take his dad's Thunderbird?" Amy asked. She had been pumping Maria all afternoon for details about the night before, but with little success. Maria was in one of her quieter, more thoughtful moods.

"Yeah," she replied, staring into the white haze over the water. "It's a real dreamy car. Like something in a magazine."

"I think Stuart really digs you," Amy said, turning her eyes to Maria's.

"Well . . . I guess I dig him, too," Maria replied after a long while. "He's a little immature, but — "

"All boys are immature," Amy interrupted. She bent down to pick up a clamshell.

Maria gazed straight ahead at the mysterious beach house a few hundred yards in front of them. The white, hazy afternoon light made the house seem even darker than usual. The tide was coming in, and waves rushed under the house, frothing white against the stilts, then pulling back with a *whoosh*.

Suddenly, as she stared, the glass door facing the ocean slid open, and a figure came running out, running at full speed toward them. As if he had spotted them from inside the house.

"Buddy!"

Maria's stomach knotted in dread.

She hadn't looked forward to seeing him, to having to explain why she had stood him up the night before.

She knew he'd be angry. About that. And about the swim trunks.

He hated to be teased. And yesterday was much worse than teasing.

"Hey — " he called to them, waving as he ran.

Maybe I should turn and run, Maria thought in a panic. She glanced at Amy and caught a fearful expression on her face as well.

But there was nowhere to run.

Besides, that would be childish.

She had just been talking about how childish and immature boys were. She had to face him like a mature adult.

"Hi, how's it going?" he asked, his bare feet skidding to a stop a few yards in front of them. He smiled, first at Amy, then at Maria, his eyes lingering on Maria.

He was wearing a sleeveless, blue cotton T-shirt and baggy Hawaiian-style swim trunks. He had a white beach towel wrapped around his broad shoulders, which were already tanned, even though summer had just begun.

"Hi." Maria gave him a shy wave. "About last night — "

"The sun should burn through soon," he said, shielding his eyes with one hand and peering up at the bright white sky. "Have you been in the water?"

"No. Brrrrr," Amy replied, wrapping her hands around her shoulders, pretending to shiver.

"No. The water's really warm," Buddy said, gripping the ends of the towel around his neck with both hands. "I guess because the air is cold."

Maria waited for him to return his eyes to her.

Was he avoiding her?

Was he so angry at her that he planned to ignore her?

No.

He reached out and swatted a green fly off her

shoulder. "Look out. The green ones bite."

"They sprayed the beach and the dunes with DDT last week," Amy said.

"But it only kills the mosquitoes. Not the flies," Buddy told her.

"About last night," Maria said, practically bursting to make her phony excuse. "I'm really sorry, Buddy."

His brown eyes narrowed, but his easy, relaxed expression remained. "Hey, I thought we were going to go into town and mess around," he said casually.

"Yeah. I know." Maria glanced at Amy, who turned her eyes to the ocean. "I wanted to. But I wasn't feeling very well. Too much sun."

She studied his face, trying to determine if he was believing her at all. If only I were a better liar, she thought. Maria could hear her voice trembling guiltily, and she knew that she was blushing. "I tried to call you — " she started to add.

"There's no phone in the beach house," he interrupted, gesturing back to the shadowy structure perched over the shore.

"No phone?" Amy asked, feeling it was safe to return to the conversation.

"The phone lines don't go that far. The house is out of the town's limits or something." He turned back to Maria, his face filled with concern. "Are you feeling better?"

She nodded, feeling even more guilty. "Yeah. I'm really sorry about last night."

"Hey. No big deal," he said, shrugging. "I'm just glad you're feeling okay."

Maria stared at him, studying his dark features, surprised by his casual reaction to being stood up.

I guess he believes me, she thought. Maybe I'm not such a bad liar after all.

"Sorry about yesterday," Amy said. "You know. The swim trunks and everything." Her gray-blue eyes twinkled, and she was unable to keep a mischievous grin from spreading across her pale face.

"Amy and I tried to get your trunks away from the boys," Maria said quickly. "How did you get back?"

"I swam," Buddy said, frowning.

Maria thought she detected a flash of anger in his eyes, but it quickly faded.

"I swam to my house," he said, gesturing with his head to the beach house. "Then I just ran inside. No big deal."

"But that was a long swim," Amy insisted. "We were way down there, by the lifeguard station." She pointed.

"Luckily the current was going my way," Buddy explained, tugging the towel behind his neck first one way, then the other. "I sort of floated most of the way, just let it carry me."

"That was a dumb joke," Maria said, shaking her head, then nervously tugging at her black ponytail. "Sometimes Ronnie and Stuart — "

"I was pretty cold when I finally got out," Buddy admitted. "But, hey — I'll pay them back." He laughed. Mirthless laughter. Not as casual as he had intended.

Amy tossed the clamshell into the water.

"How about a swim?" Buddy asked suddenly, tossing the towel to the sand.

"It's awfully cold without the sun," Maria said, glancing up at the white glare of the sky.

"It's pretty foggy out there," Amy said.

"The water's real warm, and the waves are gentle," Buddy replied. "Come on. I'll show you."

"I can't," Amy said, glancing at Maria. "I promised I'd take care of my little sister. I'm late already."

"I'll come with you," Maria said quickly.

"No. Stay. Come on. We'll have last night's date today," Buddy urged, grabbing Maria's arm gently.

"Well . . ."

"Yeah. Stay," Amy urged, starting down the beach. "I'm really gonna catch it if I don't hurry. Call you later, Maria." With a wave to them both, she began running across the beach, the man's shirt that she wore over her bathing suit flapping behind her like Superman's cape.

Maria watched Amy until she appeared to be swallowed up by the encroaching fog. Then she turned to Buddy, who was still holding her arm. "You sure you want to swim?"

He nodded, staring into her eyes. "Yeah. Come on. It'll be great. Just the two of us." His expression remained earnest, but his dark eyes suddenly seemed alive, excited.

"I'm not that good a swimmer," Maria admitted, following him as he jogged to the water's edge.

"Look how calm it is," he said, pointing.

The waves were low, lapping softly against the sand before sliding back with a gentle *whoosh*.

"Amazing!" Maria exclaimed softly. "It almost looks like a lake." She took a few steps into the water, the surf rolling over her ankles, her feet sinking into the sand as she walked. "Ooh — I thought you said it was *warm!*"

Buddy laughed. He was several steps ahead of her, in up to his knees. "You'll get used to it." He came back quickly, taking both her hands and pulling her out deeper.

"Oh!" Maria cried out from the shock of the cold.

She pulled her hands from his and dived under the water. The only way to get used to it is to get in fast, she thought. Surfacing, she looked for him. He had been right ahead of her. Where had he disappeared to?

"Right here!" he called from behind.

She spun around in the water, disoriented.

There was more of an undertow than she had thought.

"I got turned around," she explained, swimming to him.

"Let's go out further and get away from the undertow," he said. He ducked under the water, then surfaced, taking long, steady strokes, gliding easily.

He's a really good swimmer, Maria thought. She found herself to be a little surprised. He had always seemed so awkward, almost clumsy, on shore.

She did pretty well in the water, considering she'd only had a few months of Red Cross lessons at the Y, and had never really gotten to swim except during her family vacations in Dunehampton. She was probably a better swimmer than she'd realized. She just didn't have much confidence.

"Hey — we're getting pretty far from shore!" she called to Buddy.

But he didn't react, didn't seem to hear her. He was several yards ahead of her now, swimming straight and fast despite the roll and sway of the water.

"Hey — Buddy!" Maria called.

He kept swimming, his arms stretching out in those long, regular strokes, his face turned away from her.

"Buddy!"

Her arms ached. She floated for a moment, catching her breath.

"Buddy — too far!"

The fog seemed to swirl about her. She turned back. The shore was a faint outline, buried in haze . . so far away.

The dark water offered the only color out here. Everything else was gray and white, the white glare of the sky, the gray fog . . . circling her, circling her.

"Buddy!" she screamed.

Where was he?

Was she all alone out here?

All alone in the fog?

The water rolled and tilted, tossing her one way, then another.

I'm dizzy, she thought.

And then she scolded herself: Don't panic.

You're a good swimmer. And you're not really that far from shore.

The fog just makes it seem farther.

The white glare and the fog.

She closed her eyes for a moment, swimming hard.

"Buddy!"

And there he was. At her side.

"What's wrong?" He flashed her a reassuring smile. He wasn't even out of breath.

"I — I didn't see you." She held onto his shoulder, which was surprisingly muscular. He had never seemed very strong on shore.

"Here I am." She had never seen him smile so broadly, so easily. He seemed so *happy* out here.

But she was frightened now. Of the fog. Of how far they'd swum.

"I want to go back, Buddy."

He lowered his lips in a pout, playful but seriously disappointed. "Just a little farther. The water's so great today."

She realized that she was still gripping his shoulder. "I'm cold. And I'm worried."

His eyes widened.

They both bobbed as a current carried them to the side. It felt cold, colder than the water that remained behind it.

"We're not that far," he said, gazing back to shore.

"There were sharks. Remember? Not too far out," she said.

"Sharks won't bother you," he said, his expression a blank, his dark eyes suddenly dull. "Unless they smell blood."

Was he trying to scare her? To be funny?

Why did he say that?

"No. Really," she said, and then sputtered as she swallowed a mouthful of water.

When she stopped choking, trying to spit out the salty taste, he was swimming again, pulling himself further out, deeper into the swirling, heavy grayness of the low fog.

"No — Buddy — wait!"

He stopped his stroke, floated, waited for her to catch up.

"Buddy — really. I want to go back now. I'm not that good a swimmer."

To her surprise, his expression had completely changed. It was as if all the warmth had floated away. He stared at her with cold, narrowed eyes.

He grabbed her shoulder. Hard.

"I'm going to take care of you," he said. Without warmth or concern.

"What?" Was he trying to reassure her? That didn't seem to be his intention.

Was he trying to *scare* her? Why would he do that?

"Buddy — I'm going back now."

"No. You're not. I'm going to take care of you, Maria."

Reading his expression, she gasped. "Let go of me!"

4
Hurt Feelings

"Let go!" Maria repeated.

Buddy released his grip and gave her a hard shove.

She felt suddenly heavy, heavy with fear. So heavy, she felt that she might sink, just drop out of sight to the bottom of the ocean and never come up.

Why was he glaring at her like that?

What had she *done*?

"You hurt my feelings," he said, as if answering her question.

A strong current raised them both up toward the graying sky, swirled them around. Thick wisps of fog lowered around them, floating toward the shore.

I'm dreaming, Maria thought. This is a bad dream.

I can't be out in the ocean in the hazy fog, so far from shore, with this boy so filled with anger, with hatred.

"Buddy — it was a joke!" she shouted, pleading, her fear choking the sound of her voice. Again, she swallowed a mouthful of water, salty and thick. She coughed, cleared her throat. "We were just joking!"

"*It was no joke!*" he screamed, anger tightening his features. "*You hurt my feelings.*"

"Well, I'm sorry," she said, turning her eyes to shore. The beach had been swallowed up by the haze. She couldn't tell where the water ended and the land began.

How far out *am* I? she wondered.

Can I make it back by myself?

She realized she was trembling. From the cold? From her fear?

Buddy turned away from her sharply and, with long, steady strokes, swam further out, gliding through the bobbing water.

"No. Buddy — come back!" Maria pleaded. "Please!"

Should she swim after him?

Should she turn toward shore? Try to get back without his help?

She stared through the fog. If only she could see how far from shore she had swum.

If only she weren't so frightened.

He had seemed like such a nice guy. Quiet. Serious.

"Hey!"

He popped up beside her, shouting in her ear.

Startled, she uttered a short cry. "You scared me."

"I know."

"Buddy — stop. You're really scaring me. I want to go back now."

"I know."

"You're not funny," she said, trying to hold herself together, trying to hold back the loud sobs that were welling in her chest, trying to keep the tears from bursting from her eyes.

"I know."

"Stop saying that!" she screamed. "Come on — I'm cold, and I'm frightened."

"I know."

He stared at her, unblinking, silently treading water, his breathing steady, calm.

He's crazy, she thought.

She dived under a sloping wave, turned, and came up facing the shore.

At least she *thought* she was facing the shore. The fog had thickened, had formed a wall between her and the beach.

I don't even know which way to swim, she realized, feeling so heavy now, her arms so heavy, her legs. She had to force herself to keep breathing.

The sky, the gray, hazy sky, seemed low enough to reach up and touch. The wall of fog circled, closed in.

Everything was closing in on her.

Her own heart seemed to close in, to tighten.

"Buddy — what are you going to do? My arms are tired. I can't keep floating like this."

"You hurt my feelings," he repeated, staring

hard into her eyes. For the first time, she noticed a slender scar on his chin, like a tiny, white snake catching the white glare of the sky.

"Buddy — can we go back and dry off and talk about it on the beach?" she begged, her voice high and tight, a voice she'd never heard before.

He ignored her question. "You lied to me, Maria."

"Huh?"

I can't breathe, she thought.

I can't breathe, and I can't move my arms.

"I know you went out with Stuart last night."

"I'm sorry, Buddy. Really. I am. But you have to take me back now. *You have to take me back!*"

"I just hate to be lied to," he said flatly, his face expressionless.

Maria suddenly realized he wasn't staring at her. His gaze was over her shoulder, past her in the rolling waters. She turned to see what had caught his eye.

Dark shapes. Skimming rapidly along the surface of the water.

Like submarines. Dark triangles moving silently toward them.

Buddy returned his eyes to hers.

She saw the smile form on his face. The strangest smile.

"Sharks," he said.

5
Where Is Buddy?

Maria took another glance at the approaching black triangles, gliding so quickly, so easily over the water toward them.

The strange smile hadn't faded from Buddy's face. His eyes glowed, almost gleefully.

Choked with panic, Maria turned and began thrashing toward shore. Her arms ached. Her legs kicked wildly.

I don't want to die.

I don't want to die.

Was she swimming in the right direction?

Was she moving?

She couldn't tell which way the current was pulling her. Surrounded by the thick, wet fog, she couldn't even see which way to swim.

"Buddy — help me!"

She wasn't even sure it was she who was screaming — screaming Buddy's name again and again as the dark triangles swam closer, deadly shadows against the white fog wall.

"Buddy! Buddy!'

Thrashing in panic, kicking out frantically, she held her breath, dived down, tried to stroke normally, then emerged, gasping for breath.

And felt a hand grip her arm.

"Buddy!"

Water poured down her face, so cold, so salty.

And when her burning eyes cleared, his strange smile was close to her face.

She pulled away. Or tried to. But he had her in a powerful, one-handed grip.

And in his other hand?

She struggled to focus.

Her eyes blurred by the saltwater, by her panic.

The fog seemed to be inside her head now, descending, blocking out her thoughts, as thick as the fog that surrounded her in the tossing waters.

And when her eyes finally cleared, she saw the small, red-handled knife in his hand.

Knife?

She thrashed harder. But he wouldn't let go.

Knife?

"Buddy!"

Yes. A knife.

She gasped, swallowing water, choking, spitting.

"Buddy — the knife!"

His voice was so calm, so cold and calm. "The sharks won't attack without blood, Maria."

He slashed her arm, the blade digging deep into

her flesh. The dark liquid poured into the water.

She cried out as the pain ran up her arm, cutting through the fog in her mind.

The pain shot through her entire body, as fast as sharks through water.

And then another stab of pain. And another.

As Buddy stabbed her. And slashed her.

And it was hard to tell where the blood stopped and the ocean began.

"Shark food." She thought she heard him say that.

And she thought she heard him laugh. A high-pitched, crazy giggle.

"Shark food."

Yes. He repeated it.

So calm. So cold.

And then she heard his high-pitched laugh again. And she heard him call: "See you later, alligator." He sounded so . . . happy.

Then, he was gone.

Thrashing, choking, she felt herself sink, pulled down into her own blood, down, down into the cold, swirling darkness.

Buddy made his way easily to shore. Running onto the beach just a few yards from the beach house, a dark, hovering square against the steamy fog, he turned back to the water.

Shielding his eyes from the glare with both hands, he searched for Maria.

No.

No sign of her.

Gone.

"Shark food."

He said it aloud a few more times.

It was funny, actually.

He realized he was shivering.

The thrill of it was wearing off, and now he was just cold.

The excitement wasn't quite what he had expected. Sure, it was thrilling, he thought.

Sure, it was really *neat*.

But the thrill of it had worn off already.

And now he felt . . .

What did he feel?

Nothing. Nothing at all.

Just cold and wet. And eager to get home.

He scanned the dark water one more time. No sign of her.

Then, shivering hard, he picked up the towel he had left on the sand. Draping it over his shoulders, he jogged to the beach house.

He climbed up the four steps to the deck, then walked around to the sliding-glass door, not the slightest bit out of breath. He slid the door open, stepped quickly inside, then carefully slid it closed behind him.

Dunehampton police officers, in their knee-length black shorts and black, short-sleeved uniform shirts, covered the beach like dark seabirds, poking everywhere, eyes darting along the shoreline, their radios crackling. Police from two neighboring towns had been called to join the search.

A dark Coast Guard ship prowled the waters offshore, slicing through the early evening fog. From shore, the ship seemed to drift in and out of the haze, a ghostly shadow on the horizon.

"They won't find her," Amy said miserably, wiping tears from her eyes with both hands. "She can't still be swimming. She has to be dead."

"She wasn't a very good swimmer," Stuart said sadly, hands shoved into the pockets of his tan Bermuda shorts. "She told me so."

"I can't believe we're talking about Maria in the past tense," Ronnie said, his voice breaking with emotion.

Normally, Stuart loved to imitate Ronnie when his voice cracked like that. But now he didn't raise his eyes from the sand.

The three friends continued walking aimlessly along the drab, cold, fog-ridden beach, watching the policemen, hoping against hope that Maria might show up alive.

"It's so gray," Amy said. "Everything is gray — the sand, the sky, the water." She uttered a loud sob and covered her face with her hands. "I can't believe I was standing right here with Maria. Less than a few hours ago we were walking here, kidding around. And we had no idea that in a few hours, Maria would be — "

She sobbed again. She didn't want to finish her sentence.

Ronnie stooped over and put an arm around her shoulder, his yellow windbreaker flapping in the wind off the ocean.

"As long as her body isn't found, there's still hope," Stuart said. But his quavering voice showed that even he didn't believe that.

"You know what I feel bad about?" Ronnie asked, still holding Amy. She pressed her face against the front of his shirt to muffle her sobs, her shoulders bobbing up and down.

"What?" Stuart asked, staring out at the shadowy Coast Guard ship.

"We were so mean to Buddy."

"Yeah." Ronnie kicked at the wet sand. "We weren't too nice to him, were we?" he said regretfully. "He wasn't such a bad guy."

"Yeah," Stuart agreed softly.

Amy pushed herself from Ronnie, rubbing away the tears that streaked down her cheeks, which were red and swollen from crying. "I think I'm all cried out," she said, her chin trembling. "It — it's just so strange. I can still picture Maria and Buddy standing here. They can't be dead. They *can't* be!"

"Buddy was a real good swimmer," Stuart said thoughtfully. "He was a real champ. Something bad must have happened out there. I just don't understand — "

They were interrupted by a solemn-faced, young policeman, who came jogging up to them, his black high-top Keds squishing over the sand. He was boyishly handsome, with a short blond flattop and clear blue eyes.

He looks like Tab Hunter, Amy thought. And then scolded herself: How can I be thinking about movie stars at a time like this?

"Sorry to bother you," the policeman said in a surprisingly deep voice. "I'm Officer Barrett. I'm stationed in Westhaven."

"Hi," Stuart said uncomfortably, staring at the silver badge pinned over the pocket of the young policeman's short-sleeved shirt. Poking out of the pocket was a pack of Old Gold cigarettes.

The others nodded silently at the officer. Amy reached for Ronnie's hand. "Do you have bad news?" she asked reluctantly.

Barrett shook his head. "No. I just wondered if you'd repeat a few things. I know you told your story to someone from the Dunehampton station. But I'd just like to double-check."

Amy breathed a sigh of relief, but held tightly to Ronnie's hand. "They haven't found them?" she asked.

The policeman shook his head again. "It's real foggy. Can't see very far. No sign of anything on the beach. The Coast Guard spotted a number of sharks pretty close in to shore, but — "

"Sharks?" Amy cried, her eyes wide with alarm.

The policeman blushed, realizing he'd made a mistake. "Nothing to be alarmed about," he said quickly, shifting his weight uncomfortably, staring at Amy over the notepad in his hand. "I mean, it's pretty normal to see sharks this time of year. I mean — " He cleared his throat and turned his eyes to the notepad. "You say you saw her go off this morning with a boy named Buddy?" he asked, lowering his voice, assuming a more businesslike tone.

"Yeah," Amy said, nodding.

"Did you see the two of them go into the water?"

"No," Amy replied. "I left. I had to go take care of Mary Ann. My little sister. But I know Buddy *wanted* to go swimming. He wanted all three of us to — " She shivered, realizing that if she had stayed, she might have drowned with them.

"But you didn't actually see them go swimming?" Barrett demanded, locking his blue eyes on Amy.

"No," Amy said uncertainly. "Not actually. Do you think — ?"

Barrett shrugged his broad shoulders. "Your guess is as good as mine." He glanced back at the pad. "And no one knows this Buddy's last name?"

None of them did.

"His parents haven't called the police to report him missing or anything," Barrett told them. "Do you know Buddy's parents?"

Again, none of them did.

I've never seen his parents, Amy thought.

"Maybe they're away for the day or something," Barrett said, rapidly jotting a note in his pad. "Maybe they don't know he's missing. Now, tell me again where Buddy and his family are staying."

"Right up there," Stuart said, pointing to the dark beach house. All four of them turned their eyes to the house. When the tide was out, the stilts underneath looked even more like legs.

"I'm going to take a look over there," Barrett told them. "Thanks for your help."

"Is it okay if we come, too?" Ronnie asked, squeezing Amy's hand.

"I guess," Barrett replied, starting to jog toward the beach house. "Just keep out of the way. And don't touch a thing."

Four steps led up to a wooden deck that circled the house. A sliding-glass door faced the ocean. Barrett pulled the handle with both hands. The door slid open easily, and they stepped inside.

"Anybody home?" Barrett called.

Silence.

Even with the doors and windows closed, the steady wash of the ocean filled the house. "Like being on a boat," Barrett muttered, his eyes surveying the living room.

Amy and the two boys stood in the doorway. From there they could see the big living room, with its sloping cathedral ceiling, and, beyond it, the bright, pale green kitchen. A hallway at the far wall led to the bedrooms in back.

The living room was sparsely furnished, they saw. The furniture was very modern-looking. A pastel-green and blue vinyl couch with wrought-iron legs stood against one wall behind a low, oval-shaped, glass and wrought-iron coffee table. A very low, canvas chair stood at an angle to the couch beside a chrome floor lamp. Bookshelves made of white two-by-fours and red bricks lined the wall. But the shelves were empty.

The house, Amy saw, was empty.

No magazines or newspapers on the coffee table.

No food, no dirty dishes or glasses on the pale rose-colored Formica kitchen counter.

No bathing suits or beach towels tossed on the floor.

The couch cushions were perfectly smooth, as if no one had ever sat on them.

Nothing out of place. No sign of anyone.

"Stay here," Barrett ordered. "I'll be right back."

He disappeared into the hallway, and they could hear him walking around on the uncarpeted floors. "Big closet," they heard him mutter from the front bedroom.

He reappeared a few seconds later, scratching his short blond hair, shaking his head.

"No clothes," he told them. "No suitcases. No toothbrush in the bathroom." He walked past them into the kitchen and pulled open the refrigerator. "Empty."

"But we saw him — " Amy started.

He pulled open the cabinet door under the sink. No waste basket. No cleaning supplies.

He pulled open the broom closet. Empty. He opened the door on the white enamel oven. Spotless inside.

"No one lives here," Barrett said, giving Amy a suspicious stare. "Look at this place. It's untouched. No one has *ever* lived here."

"But we saw him come out of this house!" Amy protested. "Maria and I. This morning."

"Yeah. Buddy *told* us he was staying here," Ronnie told the policeman.

Barrett narrowed his eyes and scowled at them. "Buddy lied."

PART TWO

This Summer

6
Carried Away

"Wow! Is this beautiful or what?" Ashley declared.

She slid to the bottom of the dune and stared across the crowded beach to the ocean, sparkling under the brilliant afternoon sun as if lit by millions of tiny diamonds.

Dragging his yellow Styrofoam boogie board across the sand, Ross came up beside her. "Ow! The sand is *hot* here. Let's go closer to the water."

Ashley twisted her pretty face into an expression of mock sympathy. "Oooh, the little feet are too hot?" she asked in a sarcastic baby voice.

Ross scowled, furrowing his dark eyebrows. "The sand is *hot*, Ashley. You don't have to make fun of me."

"Yes, I do," she replied, giving him a playful shove that sent him toppling into the side of the dune. "It's my hobby."

"Well, get a new hobby," he said, not smiling.

He used the boogie board to help pull himself up and brushed sand off his orange Day Glo baggies. "Why not take up aerobics or something and get off my case?"

"Hey — " She put a hand tenderly on his tanned shoulder and pushed her lips into a pout. "You think I need exercise or something?" She took a step back and struck a pose for him.

Ashley was thin and beautiful, and knew it. She had very fine, straight, silvery-blonde hair, high cheekbones, and striking green eyes over a perfect, straight nose and delicate, heart-shaped lips.

She looked like a model in *Seventeen* or *Sassy* and, in fact, she had done some fashion modeling back home in Ridgefield. She also knew that the chartreuse bikini she was wearing was a knockout.

"I didn't say you need exercise," Ross insisted, smiling finally. "I said you needed a different hobby. Something better than picking on me. Why don't you go save the rain forests or something?"

"Why don't *you*?" she snapped back. "I think teasing you is a perfectly good hobby. Keeps you from getting a swelled head."

Ross didn't reply. Instead, he tugged at the handle of his boogie board and started down toward the water.

"Hey — wait up!" Ashley had to jog to keep up with him.

They made their way past a fast and furious volleyball game. A boom box resting on an enormous

Mickey Mouse beach blanket blared rap music.

"Keep going," Ashley instructed, putting a hand on Ross's shoulder. "I think I see Lucy and Kip."

"Don't you think Kip looks like Vanilla Ice?" Ross asked, picking up the boogie board and making his way between two tilting beach umbrellas.

"He's trying," Ashley said dryly.

Ross stopped suddenly. "You're glad you came?"

Ashley smiled at him. "Yeah. Somehow I couldn't get too pumped about spending the day on a smelly fishing boat with Mom and my two brothers."

His dark eyes peered into hers. "Were they crying their eyes out because you decided to come with me?"

"Not exactly," Ashley admitted. "In fact, I think Robin's exact words were, 'Who cares?' "

She expected him to laugh, but his expression turned thoughtful. Ross looks just like Matt Dillon, Ashley thought. The straight black hair and heavy eyebrows, the intense, serious face.

She smiled and gave the lifeguard, a beefy blond with bright red cheeks, a friendly wave as they walked in front of the tall, white, wooden chair.

Ross scowled. "Hey — don't flirt with him. How could you come on to a guy who looks like that?"

Ashley turned angrily. "You *said* you weren't going to be so jealous all the time, Ross."

He shrugged. "You promised you wouldn't come on to every guy on the beach."

"I didn't come on to him. I just smiled. Are you

going to keep your promise or not?"

"Yeah. Okay," he muttered, avoiding her stare. "Sorry."

"Hey — there's Lucy and Kip. On that big MTV blanket. Over there. See?" She waved to Lucy, but Lucy was talking to Kip and didn't see her.

"Look at him," Ross urged, hurrying to keep up with her. "Vanilla Ice. Right?"

"On a bad day," she muttered.

"You don't like Kip, do you?"

Ashley shook her head. "I think he's mean. He's not very nice to Lucy. And he has no sense of humor at all."

Ross started to say something, but they had reached Lucy's blanket. Lucy was lying on her stomach beside Kip, but she jumped up, adjusting her bikini top, to greet the two arrivals. She had curly auburn hair, a face full of freckles, and enormous blue eyes.

"Hey — how's it going?" Kip asked, reaching for a bottle of suntan lotion.

"Isn't this a gorgeous day?" Lucy said excitedly. She had a slight lisp, which made her sound like a little girl. Lucy didn't mind. Most boys thought it was really cute.

Lucy never had any trouble attracting boys, which made Ashley really wonder why she chose to hang out with this tough-looking townie, Kip.

Ross propped the boogie board up in the sand and dropped down next to Kip on the beach towel. "What number is that?" he asked, pointing to the lotion Kip was slathering onto his narrow, white shoulders.

"Two hundred and twelve, I think," Kip replied, squeezing more from the bottle. "I need a lot of protection." The diamondlike stud in his ear glinted in the sun.

"Did you quit your job?" Ashley asked Kip, trying to be friendly for Lucy's sake. Kip's summer job was driving an ice-cream truck from beach to beach.

"No. My day off. The little animals will have to get their ice cream from someone else today." He rolled onto his side, turning his back on the others.

"I'm so jealous of you," Lucy said to Ashley.

"Huh?" Ashley reacted with surprise. "What are you talking about?"

"You get to stay here and party all summer. I have to go back to Ridgefield in two weeks." Lucy slapped at a green fly on her leg.

"Bummer," Kip muttered without turning around.

"Maybe you could stay with us," Ashley said, kicking off her rubber thongs. "There's an extra guestroom at the house we're renting. I could ask my parents."

"No, I can't," Lucy said, shaking her head. "I'm taking the second term of summer school, remember? A little brushup on the French I practically flunked last spring."

"Well, we'll just have to make sure it's a great two weeks," Ashley said enthusiastically. She turned her gaze down the crowded beach. A few brave souls had ventured into the water, little children, mostly. But even with the June sun burning down, the water still was cold enough to make your ankles ache.

Her eyes came to rest on the old beach house jutting into the water on stilts at the end of the beach. Who ever decided to build a house there? she wondered, as she had been wondering every summer since her family had started coming to Dunehampton. There were no other houses on the beach, certainly not right in the water.

And why hadn't the house ever been sold or rented?

She and Ross had walked over to it a few nights before. They had found it as dark and empty as in previous years. The redwood walls had been darkened nearly to black by the moisture and salt in the air. The floorboards of the deck had started to rot, and a window pane in one of the bedrooms had shattered, leaving a gaping hole.

The house is kind of sad and creepy, Ashley thought. She wished someone would tear it down.

"Could you get us some free Fudgsicles from your truck tomorrow?" Ross asked Kip. "Or maybe some toasted almond bars?"

To everyone's surprise, Kip spun around and sat up, glaring at Ross angrily. "Hey, man, are you putting me down because I have to work this summer?"

"Whoa — " Ross started, raising both hands as

if to shield himself. He edged away from Kip on the blanket.

But Kip wouldn't let Ross get a word in. "You think it's some kind of a joke because I have to wear a stupid uniform and sell stupid ice cream while you lie on the beach all day?" he raged, his pale face reddening, his hands balled into tight fists.

"Whoa — " Ross jumped to his feet. "I wasn't putting you down," he insisted heatedly. "I've had summer jobs before. I work after school. My dad was laid off for over a year, Kip."

Kip scowled and looked away.

"I was just kidding around," Ross said, glancing at Ashley.

"Well, don't kid around," Kip snapped, but his angry tone had softened. "I don't like kidding around." And then he added, "Unless I'm doing the kidding." A weak joke, but at least he was trying to show Ross that he wasn't still angry.

"You've got to watch out for Kip," Lucy added with a phony laugh, trying to keep things light. "He's a *baad dude*."

"You summer people come here and think you own the place," Kip grumbled, ignoring Lucy. "Meanwhile, the rest of us are here all winter, just trying to hang on. Just hanging on."

He dropped back down on the big MTV beach blanket, again turning his back on them. "You like the blue Italian ice, comes in a cup?" he asked Ross quietly.

"Yeah. I guess," Ross replied.

"I can probably get you some of those. It's my worst seller."

"Ugh. Blue food," Ashley said, making a face. "What flavor is it?"

"Blue," Kip told her.

Ashley started to protest that blue wasn't a flavor. But her words caught in her throat as a hulking figure spun her around from behind.

She screamed as he picked her up in his powerful arms, his long, black hair wild about his face, his eyes wide with excitement, his mouth fixed in a determined grin.

Lucy leapt back in surprise, covering her mouth with her hands.

Ross and Kip struggled to their feet.

But they were too late.

The enormous intruder was running off with Ashley, carrying her toward the water.

"Help!" Ashley screamed. "Ross — help! *Please!*"

7
Ashley's Fear

"Ross — help me!"

Ashley's pleas for help were drowned out by an openmouthed roar from her captor. She struggled to free herself, pounding his broad chest with her fists, but he held her tightly, running rapidly to the water.

His feet were splashing up water now.

Roaring at the top of his lungs, he carried her straight into a crashing wave.

"Let go!" she shrieked.

And he did.

And Ashley plummeted into the freezing cold water, sputtering and thrashing her arms and legs.

Her feet found the sandy bottom. She stood. Ducked under a wave.

Then leapt at her captor, shoving his shoulders. "Denny — you're an animal!" she screamed, shoving him again.

Denny Drake laughed. "You looked hot, Ashley.

I thought maybe you needed to cool off."

Struggling to stay afloat, she splashed him with one hand. "And you know what *you* need? You need a *keeper!*"

He laughed again, enjoying his triumph.

Denny had grown up a few houses down from Ross back in Ridgefield. He wasn't really a friend. But he always seemed to be around.

A tall, muscular guy with big shoulders and a well-developed chest, Denny could have been a stand-in for the Incredible Hulk. In fact, that was his nickname back at Ridgefield High — Hulkster.

"You and I have *got* to stop meeting like this, Ashley," he joked, giving her a final splash before hauling himself out of the water.

"Shut up, Denny," she shouted. "You got my new bathing suit all wet!"

He laughed again, shaking his long hair like a dog after a bath. "You *love* it. Why don't you lose that wimp and go to the six-plex with me tonight?" He gestured toward Ross, who was still back with the others, all three of them laughing at Ashley's abduction.

Ashley came running out of the water, moving quickly past Denny, heading toward her friends. "You're joking — right?"

"Huh-uh." Denny shook his head.

"Go *out* with you? That's your funniest joke yet."

Denny's expression changed. He looked hurt. "Thanks for the swim." He snarled and clomped away.

Lucy came running with a towel for Ashley. She dried Ashley's hair and shoulders, then draped it around her. "Denny really is a beast," Ashley muttered.

"I think he likes you," Lucy said seriously.

"Thrills and chills," was Ashley's sarcastic reply.

When they got back to the MTV blanket, Ashley was surprised to see that they had been joined by a new boy, someone she had never seen before. He was tall and good-looking, with wavy dark hair and a shy smile. He was wearing blue spandex trunks, very tight, and a red and white Grateful Dead T-shirt, several sizes too big.

"How was the water?" Kip asked, chuckling.

"Just great," Ashley told him. "You should try it."

"You gonna *carry* me in?" Kip teased.

Ashley made a face at him, sticking out her tongue. She searched her bag and pulled out a dry towel. Then she turned to the new boy. "Hi."

"This is Brad," Ross said to Ashley. He shrugged at Brad. "Sorry. I forgot your last name."

"Brad Sayles," the boy replied, keeping his dark eyes on Ashley. "Ross and I took tennis lessons together last summer. Remember — we had that instructor who couldn't serve the ball over the net?"

"Yeah. He was a real winner," Ross said. "He couldn't serve, but he had a great follow-through. All he ever talked about was follow-through."

"Are you a townie?" Ashley asked, embarrassed by the way Brad was staring at her. She wrapped the towel around her waist like a sarong.

"No," Brad said, smiling as if Ashley had made a joke. "We live in Cambridge. But my family has always had a house here. On Ocean Drive."

"Ocean Drive?" Kip exclaimed. He had been drowsing, but the two words snapped him back to life. "You mean where all the big mansions are?"

Standing behind the blanket, Brad shifted his weight uncomfortably. "Our house is pretty big," he said, as if confessing to a major sin. "I guess you could call it a mansion." All the while, he kept staring at Ashley, smiling at her, studying her.

"Does it have an east wing and a west wing?" Lucy asked, dropping down beside Kip. "I've always wanted a house with wings."

Brad chuckled pleasantly. "Well, there's a servants' wing. And then the rest of the house. Oh. And a guest house. And . . . a pool house."

Kip whistled appreciatively.

"Wow," Lucy said.

Brad blushed. "You guys are embarrassing me. I can't help it if my grandfather made a ton of money. I had nothing to do with it."

He's sweet, Ashley thought. She liked the way his cheeks turned pink. He's really very good-looking. And he doesn't seem at all stuck-up like some rich people. Just the opposite.

I think he likes me, she thought. The way he's staring at me, as if trying to give me a message with his eyes.

Well, I got the message, Brad.

And you know what? I'm kind of attracted to you, too.

She glanced at Ross and caught an angry expression. Ross looked quickly toward the ocean.

How can he be jealous already? Ashley thought, extremely annoyed. Aren't I even allowed to *talk* to another boy?

Ross and I have really got to discuss this, she decided.

He promised me he'd try to control his stupid jealousy. But look at him — standing there so tense, so totally bent out of shape, hovering there like a mother hen, flashing me dirty looks. And for no reason at all.

The more she thought about it, the angrier Ashley became.

She had a sudden impulse to grab Brad by the back of the head with both hands, pull his face close, and plant a long, passionate kiss on his lips.

Give Ross something to *really* be jealous about.

Instead, she dropped down onto the sand, sitting cross-legged, and motioned for Brad to sit down beside her. He obediently sat down, stretching his long legs out, leaning back on his hands.

"So you have a pool?" she asked him.

He nodded. "Yes, it's really neat. It's Olympic-sized."

"Heated, of course?"

"Of course," he said, grinning. "Do you play tennis, too, Ashley?"

"Yeah. Ross and I have been playing every morning. Before it gets too hot."

"Well, maybe you'd like to come play a few sets at my house. We have our own clay court."

"That would be excellent," Ashley replied enthusiastically. "Wouldn't it, Ross?" She glanced up. "Ross?"

Where was he?

"Hey — Ross?"

Then she saw him walking away, taking long, angry strides. Ashley jumped to her feet and called to him, cupping her hands around her mouth. "Ross, come back!"

He must have heard her. But he kept walking without turning around.

Oh, wonderful, Ashley thought, sighing. She watched him disappear over the dunes, heading for the road.

Now what have I done?

"Ross, how can you be jealous? I was just *talking* to Brad." Ashley tried to take Ross's arm, but he angrily pulled away from her.

"Ross, come *on*."

A silvery half-moon shone in the dark, hazy sky. Slivers of black cloud floated in front of it. Shadows lengthened, then shifted over the gray beach.

They were walking slowly along the edge of the dunes. Below them, ocean waves rose, dark and threatening, then crashed noisily against the sand.

The wind ruffled through Ashley's hair. She

tugged at the sleeves of the white sweatshirt she wore over black spandex leggings.

"Ross, what's your problem?"

"I *saw* the way you were looking at him," he muttered, his voice barely carrying over the roar and crash of the tumbling waves.

"I was just being friendly," Ashley replied, having to hurry to keep up with Ross's long strides. "He seemed like an okay guy. We don't have to go play on his tennis court if you don't want to."

He scowled, but didn't reply. They walked on in silence for a while.

The beach house came into view. In high tide, its stilts disappeared, and the house seemed to float on the water.

"Ross, say something. I'm getting cold. I don't want to keep walking."

He stopped and turned to her, his expression unhappy. He had his black hair tied back in a ponytail. His soulful eyes again reminded Ashley of Matt Dillon.

"Ross — say something. *Please.*"

She could see the anger spread across his face, see the hurt glow in his dark, unblinking eyes.

And suddenly she realized she was afraid of him.

He took a step toward her, his mouth frozen in an angry scowl.

Her throat tightened with fear.

She had seen him angry before. She had seen him, out of control, shove his fist through a plate-glass window.

He had the same anger now. She could almost feel it radiating from him.

This is so silly, she thought.

He's all worked up about *nothing*.

But she felt the fear just the same.

The chilling fear that if he lost his temper, he might do *anything*.

She took a step back as he moved toward her.

What was he going to do?

8
Into the Beach House

"I thought we were going to spend a great summer together," Ross finally said, standing very close to her, so close that she could practically feel the tension and anger in his body.

Ashley breathed a silent sigh of relief. At least he was keeping it under control. He wasn't going to hurt her.

He never had.

Why had she suddenly felt so afraid of him?

Maybe *I'm* the one who's losing it, she thought.

"Yes. Well — " she started.

"It was supposed to be just you and me this summer. But first you let Denny carry you into the water — "

"*Let* him?!" Ashley cried. "I didn't have much choice, did I? He came at me like a charging bull. And I didn't exactly see you come running to my rescue!"

Ross ignored her impassioned defense.

"Will you get serious?" Ashley cried. "You don't really believe I'm interested in Denny, do you?"

" — And then you start coming on to that wimpy rich kid," Ross continued, avoiding her eyes. "In front of everyone."

Now he's totally gone bananas, Ashley thought bitterly. She hated this jealousy of his, this possessiveness. It really made her furious. And afraid.

But it was also nice to know that Ross cared so much about her.

Only why did he have to be so insecure?

She *liked* to flirt with guys. It was fun.

Harmless fun.

Why couldn't Ross just lighten up once in a while?

They had discussed this before, and he'd promised that he'd try. But here they were discussing it again.

Oh, well. Ashley knew there was one quick way to end the discussion.

She reached up and grabbed his shoulders. And pulled him to her. And kissed him. A long, passionate kiss.

She didn't pull her face away until they were both breathless.

She stared into his eyes. His expression had softened. He had stopped scowling at her.

Works every time, she thought.

And kissed him again. Longer this time.

"Now are you going to shape up?" she asked playfully.

He shrugged and smiled.

She shivered. "Ooh, it's so cold. I'm totally frozen."

"I have an idea," he whispered. He gestured toward the beach house just up ahead.

Ashley hadn't realized they had walked that far. They were standing a few yards from the deck that surrounded the old house. It loomed over them, a black shadow against the starless, purple night sky.

"Let's go in and warm up," Ross said, tugging at her hand, pulling her toward the wooden stairs that led up to the deck from the dunes.

"Go in? How can we?" She pulled back.

"The door's probably open. No one has ever lived here, remember? Come on, Ashley. It's bound to be warmer in there than it is out here."

She looked up at the dark windows and shivered.

"Come on," he urged, pulling her hand. We'll pretend the house is ours."

She laughed. "Who would *want* it?" But she relented and followed him up the creaking wooden steps and onto the deck.

"Careful," he warned, whispering for some reason, and pointing down toward his bare feet. "Some of the deck boards are rotting."

They made their way around to the glass door that faced the ocean. Below them, they could hear the rush of the ocean as it flowed under the house.

Is the deck swaying in the water? Ashley wondered, gripping Ross's hand tighter. Is the whole house swaying? Or is it just my imagination?

"Ross — we really shouldn't do this," she whis-

pered. She pressed her face to the glass door and
peered inside.

Blackness. It was too dark to see anything.

"There won't be any electricity or anything," she
said, backing up a step.

"So? It'll be fun," he insisted. "Our own private
place." He squeezed her hand.

Then he gripped the door handle with both hands
and tugged.

The glass door slid open easily, silently.

"Told you it'd be unlocked. Come on." He disappeared into the house.

"But, Ross — " Ashley called in. "We don't have
a flashlight or anything." She cautiously took a step
forward, then another, feeling herself swallowed up
by the darkness of the house.

"BOO!"

She gasped and nearly fell back into the open
doorway.

Ross loomed at her side, laughing. "Gotcha," he
said in her ear, holding her shoulders.

"That was mean," Ashley said, shoving him
away.

It was surprisingly warm inside. Ross slid the
door shut. As Ashley's eyes began to adjust to the
darkness, she began to make out the forms of the
few pieces of furniture in the room.

It was all old-fashioned looking. Very fifties. A
vinyl and wrought-iron couch. A low, canvas chair.
A chrome floor lamp.

She made her way across the room, the wooden

floorboards creaking, the rush of water below, and tried the lamp.

Nothing.

"You're not afraid to be alone with me in the dark, are you?" Ross teased, stepping up behind her, leaning against her, slipping his arms around her waist.

"I'm afraid to be *anywhere* with you!" she joked. She lowered her hands and covered his. "Look at this place. It's all furnished and everything. Ready for someone to move in. But no one ever has."

"*We* have," Ross insisted, and pulled her down onto the vinyl couch.

He kissed her, wrapping his muscular arms around her, holding her tightly. "Feeling warmer?"

"A lot," she whispered. And kissed him again.

She pulled away with a start when she heard the clatter from the hallway.

They both listened.

The bedrooms must be back there, she figured.

And then she heard the clump of shoes against the floor.

And whispered voices.

"Ross — " Ashley whispered, grabbing his hand. "There's someone else in here!"

9
Murders

Ross leaned over Ashley and reached up to the lamp. He clicked it twice before he remembered there was no electricity.

The footsteps from the back hallway grew louder.

They both jumped to their feet.

A pale rectangle of moonlight spread on the floor in front of them. The ocean waves splashed noisily below the floor.

"Who's there?" Ashley called, her tight voice revealing her fear.

The footsteps stopped.

"Who's there?" she repeated, leaning against Ross.

She heard loud whispering. Then two figures appeared, moving slowly side by side, stopping just past the hall door.

"Who is it?" a girl called. A familiar voice.

"Hey — " The voice of her companion was also familiar.

"Lucy?" Ashley cried.

Kip and Lucy moved forward to greet Ashley and Ross. All four began talking excitedly at once, laughing with relief.

"How did you find us?" Lucy asked.

"We weren't exactly looking for you," Ross said dryly.

"We discovered the house was open a few nights ago," Lucy said. "It's really awesome, isn't it?"

"It was our own private place till you two barged in," Kip said unhappily. He walked to the glass door and stared out at the ocean.

"Well, we didn't know — " Ashley started to explain to him.

"It's like being on a boat," Lucy said happily. "The house even sways a little, like a boat. I just *love* it!"

"It's a little . . . creepy," Ashley said, peering into the dark kitchen.

"I don't think so. I think it's romantic," Lucy gushed.

"Me, too," Ross said, putting an arm around Ashley's shoulder.

Kip continued to stare silently out the door. Ashley figured he was really angry that she and Ross had barged in on them like this. He's so hostile and unfriendly, she decided. Why does Lucy like him so much? "I wonder why no one lives here," she said.

"Maybe it's because of the murders," Kip declared without turning around.

"Huh? Murders?"

"There are a lot of stories," Kip said mysteriously. He finally turned back and joined them in
front of the couch. "Really gross stories. About
murders."

As Kip said this, Ashley saw his eyes light up,
his face come alive.

"Murders? Here? In this house?" Lucy asked.

"Yeah," Kip said. "You don't live here, so you
don't know the stories. But everyone in Dunehampton knows. About the murders, I mean."

"Who was murdered?" Ashley asked, crossing
her arms over her chest as if for protection.

"Teenagers," was Kip's curt reply.

The whole idea of murders in this house really
pumps him up, Ashley thought, studying Kip's
glowing eyes and his amused expression.

"Teenagers were killed here. In and around the
house."

"When?" Ross asked.

"A long time ago. Sometime in the fifties. Just
after the house was built." The amused smile spread
across Kip's face. The stud in his ear sparkled as
he stepped into the rectangle of light.

He narrowed his eyes. "They never caught
whoever did it. Never solved the mystery." He
stepped back into the darkness. "And no one has
lived here since." He snickered, looking from face
to face.

"That's really gross," Lucy said, shaking her
head.

"Ross, let's get out of here," Ashley urged, reaching for his hand. She suddenly felt thoroughly chilled again.

Ross laughed. "You're frightened because of some silly story that happened over thirty years ago?"

"It's not a story. It's true," Kip said defensively.

"The idea of kids being killed right here — it just creeps me out, that's all," Ashley said, starting toward the door.

"Hey, come on, not so fast," Ross called to her. He turned to Kip. "Tell us more about it. More details."

"No!" Ashley insisted heatedly. "I really don't like it here, Ross. I'm leaving." She slid open the door. The roar of the ocean swept into the room like an angry cry. "Bye, guys," Ashley called, stepping out.

"Later," Ross said, running after her.

As he turned to slide the door closed, he saw Kip put his arm around Lucy and lead her to the couch.

He's a weird guy, Ross thought.

Wonder why he thought those murders were so funny? . . .

Ashley waited for him on the steps. "It's late," she said, yawning. "All this fresh air makes me sleepy."

"Why do you think Kip is so weird?" Ross asked as they headed over the dunes toward the road that led to their rented houses.

"He's just got a problem because he's a townie and we're not, and he thinks we all look down on townies."

"Well, we do, don't we?" Ross joked.

She laughed, pleased that his mood had improved so much. As they walked, holding hands, they talked about Lucy and Kip and the beach house.

The half-moon was high in the sky. A few stars had poked out from the clouds. The beach was deserted. In the dark ocean, sea gulls sat on the purple water, riding the rolling waves as they slept.

Ross's parents' house, a small, white clapboard bungalow, was first along the narrow, winding road. They stopped at the walk. "I'll walk you home, then come back," Ross offered.

Ashley shook her head. "No need. You know my house is just over that hill. Go to sleep. I'll call you in the morning."

Before he could protest, she kissed him quickly, missing his mouth and bumping his chin, then turned and began jogging over the hill to her house.

The road was lined on both sides with tall, grassy reeds, tilting in the wind, brushing against each other, whispering and bending.

Ashley made her way over the low, sloping hill, the reeds leaning over the road as if reaching for her. As her house came into view, she slowed to a walk.

And someone leapt out of the tall reeds to her right and grabbed her from behind.

10
Disappeared

With an anguished cry, Ashley struggled to free herself. But her attacker held her around the waist in an unbreakable grip.

She flailed out her arms and tried to kick.

He laughed and spun her around to face him.

"Denny!" she cried, her voice hoarse from her terror. "Denny — you *animal*!"

He leered at her, bringing his beefy, perspiring face close to hers. "Did I scare you?"

Furiously she swung her hand in an attempt to slap him. But he caught her hand inches from his face and held it.

"Hey, I was just goofing," he said, sounding hurt.

"I'm going to call the police. I really am," Ashley insisted. "Let *go* of my hand, Denny."

Slowly, he released her hand. She rubbed her aching wrist. Denny was stronger than even he realized.

"You could have given me a heart attack," Ashley said, her heart finally starting to resume its normal rhythm.

"I looked for you at the clambake on the beach," he said, still leering at her. He reached up a big gorilla hand and scratched the top of his head through his long, black hair.

"Ross and I didn't go," Ashley said coldly. "Who invited *you* to the clambake?"

"Nobody," he said, with some sadness. "I just crashed."

"Are you going to let me go home or what?" she snapped angrily, still rubbing her wrist. "You've done your bad deed for the night."

He pouted his lips in an exaggerated expression of hurt. "Boo-hoo. It's still early, you know."

"Well, why don't you go step on people's sandcastles or something?" Ashley said wearily, giving him a wave of dismissal with one hand.

"I already did that," he joked. A grin spread across his broad face. "I know you're hot for me," he said.

She laughed scornfully. "Denny, you've been drinking, right?"

"Admit it, Ashley," he leaned toward her menacingly.

"Yeah, I'm hot for you, Denny. Like I'm hot to have my body ripped apart by sharks."

He thought about this for a moment, eyeing her unsteadily, letting her sarcasm sink in. Then he shoved his hands into the pockets of his denim cutoffs and frowned. "Give me a break," he muttered. "I'm sorry I scared you. Really."

"Apology accepted," she said flatly.

"It's just my dumb sense of humor, you know. How about coming for a walk with me? On the beach. A short walk."

"How about not?" Ashley replied.

His eyes flared angrily for a brief moment, then quickly cooled. "I'm serious," he said softly.

"You're not serious — you're *grim*," Ashley cracked.

He glared at her, started to say something, then stopped. "Okay, Ash. See ya, kid," he muttered. He turned away and began walking up the hill, slapping at the tall reeds along the roadside as he walked.

Ashley sighed wearily. She stood watching Denny until he disappeared over the hill.

How long had she known him?

Since second grade, at least. She had never liked him all that much. Or disliked him. He had always been around. Just one of the gang.

But, now, for the first time, she realized she was frightened of him.

He's so big, she thought, turning up the flagstone walk to her house. I don't think he even realizes how strong he is.

And he seems to have so much pent-up anger. He pretends to be playful, to be goofing, kidding around. But just below the surface, he's really kind of mean.

Mean enough to hurt someone if he didn't get his way?

Ashley yawned. She was too sleepy to think about Denny now.

Besides, he was just a pest.

He didn't really mean any harm.

Ashley slept late the next morning, arising about ten-thirty. Her parents, she learned from a note on the refrigerator, had left early for the golf course.

All they care about is golf, she thought, shaking her head.

I don't know why they drag us to the beach every summer. They don't swim. They don't like to sunbathe.

Just golf, golf, golf.

She downed a quick bowl of Wheaties, threw some stuff into her beach bag, checked the batteries on her Walkman, and headed to the beach.

She was wearing her favorite new two-piece bathing suit. Very glitzy and sexy, and an amazing shade of red. It fit her fabulously, even though it looked like something Madonna might wear, and she was eager to show off.

It was a Saturday, so the beach was already crowded. She searched for her friends, wandering back and forth, stepping around blankets and beach umbrellas. No one around.

A major disappointment. I should've saved this suit till later, she thought wistfully.

She settled close to the water, spreading out her red and white Coke beach blanket. The sun kept disappearing behind high clouds, casting the crowded beach in shadow. When it emerged, it became hot and sticky. There was barely a breeze, even so close to the ocean.

Using her beach bag as a pillow, she settled back and lifted a paperback novel to her lap. She wasn't really in the mood to read, but decided she couldn't just lie there by herself, looking lonely and idle.

A few minutes later, the sun out full force again, she saw Brad walking by the shore. He was walking slowly, laughing and talking with a tall, redheaded girl, very pretty, very skinny, in a skimpy black bikini.

Ashley waved to Brad, but he didn't seem to see her.

She sat up and started to call to him, then decided not to. She felt a pang of jealousy. She realized she resented the tall redhead.

I'd like to walk on the beach with you, Brad, Ashley thought.

You're so cute.

And so rich.

Then, as if he had read her thoughts, Ross came into view.

He was several beach umbrellas down, walking slowly, stopping every few yards, his eyes surveying the crowd.

Ashley realized he must be searching for her, so

she stood up and waved. "Ross! Hey — Ross!"

He spotted her after a few seconds and came running over.

He didn't smile the way he usually did when they met.

She could see immediately that his expression was troubled.

"Hey, what's the matter?" she asked.

He mopped perspiration from his forehead with the back of his arm. She saw that he was breathing hard.

"Hi, Ashley. I — uh — "

"Ross, what's wrong?" she demanded, feeling her throat tighten in dread.

"I guess you haven't heard," he said, awkwardly standing very close to her, unable to decide what to do with his hands.

"Heard? Heard *what*?" Ashley asked impatiently.

"It's . . . Lucy and Kip," Ross said, his chin trembling. "They didn't come home last night. They've both disappeared."

PART THREE

Summer of 1956

11
Who's in the Beach House?

In Amy's dream, the blue-green water was calm at first and smooth as glass. But as she swam, farther and farther from the shore, tall waves began to toss and tumble around her.

The beach became a thin, brown line in the far distance, but she kept swimming. Face in the water. Now up for a gasping breath. Face in the water.

Stroke. Stroke. Stroke.

Her arms ached with each pull. Her legs ached, but she continued her rhythmic kicking.

Face in the water. Noisy, gasping breath.

Stroke. Stroke. Stroke.

Until even the brown line of shore disappeared from the horizon, and she was surrounded by the blue-green water, frothing white as the waves fell around her.

Surrounded by the waves, which became moving mountains, looming over her, then crashing noisily, sweeping her up in their rolling white foam.

Face in the water. Now out. Deep breath and hold it.

Stroke. Stroke. Stroke.

Until her chest felt about to burst.

And the tall waves lifted her up so that she couldn't swim any farther.

Lifted her up and held her. Held her high so that she could see the dark triangles gliding through the water, gliding so quickly, so effortlessly. While she struggled to free herself from the tall wave. While she struggled to get away.

The dark triangles riding so high in the water. Ignoring the seething waves.

"Let me go!" Amy cried.

But the wave held her high.

And the sharks closed in.

Stroke. Stroke. Stroke.

She kept moving her arms, thrashing her legs, even though the waves wouldn't let her swim.

Stroke. Stroke.

She wasn't going anywhere. And the sharks — so many sharks — so many hungry sharks — were gliding so easily, like arrows floating to their target.

Their teeth were shiny, white like pearls. Their enormous mouths opened like bottomless wells.

All together, they tore at her skin, pulling off chunks of flesh as the water darkened. Pulling at her with those gleaming white teeth, tearing away her skin as if it were paper.

And again she woke up screaming.

Again she opened her eyes to find herself bathed

in sweat, the bedclothes tangled about her bare legs. The tiny bedroom stifling. No air to breathe.

Stroke. Stroke. Stroke.

Awake, the dream followed her, stayed with her, kept its frightening rhythm.

Face in the water. Breathe. Breathe.

I can't breathe, she thought, sitting straight up in bed, her chest heaving. The room tossed about like an ocean wave.

Stroke. Stroke.

She shut her eyes tight, waited for the rolling waters to recede, for the rhythm to fade.

How many nights will I have this dream? Amy wondered.

Her heart pounding, feeling exhausted, drained, as if she had swum for miles, she pulled herself to her feet, made her way dizzily to the open window, and peered up at a pale half-moon in the purple sky.

How many nights?

She had had the dream every night since Maria and Buddy had disappeared. Every night.

"What am I going to do?" she asked the moon. "What am I going to do?"

"What am I going to do?" Amy asked, picking up a white pebble from the sand, holding it up close to examine it, then tossing it into the ocean.

"Hey, the dreams will stop after a while," Ronnie replied. But he didn't sound so sure.

High clouds covered the midmorning sun. The air carried a chill off the water. Black storm clouds on the horizon were moving quickly toward the shore.

The darkness suited Amy's mood. She adjusted the pink-and-yellow flower-patterned scarf she had tied over her tight curls. She was wearing the same tan Bermuda shorts she had worn the day before, and one of her father's old, long-sleeved white shirts, with the sleeves rolled halfway up.

She hadn't paid much attention to what she put on that morning. She really didn't care. She hadn't been able to stop thinking about Maria. Awake or asleep.

"It's going to storm," Ronnie said, shielding his eyes with one hand as he studied the horizon. Two dark ships appeared far out in the ocean, moving so slowly that they appeared to be standing still.

"I don't care," Amy said glumly. "Let it rain. I don't care if it rains for the entire summer."

"I keep thinking about Maria, too," Ronnie said, hunching down as he walked, his hands shoved into the pockets of his tennis shorts. His leather sandals slapped noisily against the hard, wet sand. "And Buddy. Buddy was such a good swimmer. I just don't understand — "

"Maybe they were attacked by sharks," Amy said, swatting at a fly on her leg. "It's the only thing I can think of. Maybe that's why I keep having that dream. Maybe — "

"I don't think we'll ever know," Ronnie said softly, putting a hand on Amy's trembling shoulder. "It's been days, and there's been no sign of them."

"That's what puzzles me," Amy said, reaching up to put her hand over his. "Where are Buddy's parents? Why haven't they contacted the police? Why hasn't anyone heard from them? Where *are* they? Don't they even *care* that their son has drowned?"

"Whoa," Ronnie said, raising a finger to his lips. "Slow down, Amy. Slow down. Take a deep breath."

She obediently took a deep breath.

"I can't help it, Ronnie. I'm just so upset!" She could feel the hot tears welling in her eyes. She wiped them away and glanced down the beach to the beach house, jutting out to the water on its fragile-looking stilts.

"It's a mystery," Ronnie agreed, running a hand back through his blond flattop as he turned to follow her gaze. "Someone should have been asking about Buddy. *Someone.*"

Thunder rumbled in the distance.

"What a *horrible* summer," Amy said, shaking her head.

They started walking, but stopped when they heard someone calling their names. Spinning around, Amy was surprised to see Stuart running toward them, waving.

"Hey — glad I found you." He stopped, putting his hands on his hips, and waited to catch his breath. His black hair was slicked down. Even the gusting storm wind off the ocean couldn't blow it out of shape. He was wearing a short-sleeved sportshirt of wide brown and yellow stripes hanging over baggy Levi's that looked stiff and new.

"Stuart, what's shaking?" Ronnie asked.

"I just came to say good-bye," he replied.

"Huh? You're leaving?" Amy reacted with surprise. She had seen Stuart once since Maria's death. He had been on his way to a barbecue with a bunch of kids. He had waved and smiled at her.

"My family is going home. My dad has to go back to the salt mines. So . . ." He shrugged.

"That's too bad," Ronnie said, shaking his head.

"What are you going to do the rest of the summer?" Amy asked, turning her eyes to the darkening sky above.

"Well, my uncle owns a drive-in back home. I'll probably work there till school starts," Stuart replied, kicking up clumps of sand with his Keds.

"You'll be a carhop?" Ronnie joked. "Do you know how to skate?"

"Yeah, I skate pretty good," Stuart bragged. "I could probably be in the Roller Derby. But I don't look so hot in the short skirts. I'll probably be manning the French fry grease pits."

"Well, good luck," Amy said.

"I'm just taking my last walk on the beach," Stuart said unhappily. "You know. Collecting some shells." His voice broke. "It's not really a summer I want to remember." He gave them a wave and headed down the beach.

Amy watched him as he walked past the beach house, stopping occasionally to pick up a shell. A short while later, he disappeared around a curve in the beach.

"Hey, look. There's a hot dog truck up on the road," Ronnie said, pointing. "I'm starving all of a sudden. Want one?"

"No. But I'll watch you eat yours," Amy said agreeably, thinking about Stuart, how funny he was, how much fun he had been — until Maria and Buddy disappeared.

Maria and Buddy.

They were gone. And everything was different now.

Everything.

They walked quickly over the grassy dune to the road.

The hot dog vendor was sitting on a folding chair inside the hot dog truck, reading the morning newspaper. He finished what he was reading, then looked up, surprised to see customers.

"You see this ship that got sunk?" he asked, holding up the front page of the paper. A photograph showed an enormous ocean liner tilted on its side. "The *Andrea Doria*," he told them. "You imagine that? A ship that big? As big as the Titanic, I'll bet. Filled with rich people. It got hit and it's sinking. You see it on TV?"

"We don't have a television here," Ronnie told him.

The man grunted, wiping his mustache with one hand. "You're gonna miss Martin and Lewis on Sunday," he said.

"Yeah. I guess." Ronnie ordered a hot dog.

Amy stood with her arms crossed, watching Ronnie gobble it down. He put mustard, relish, ketchup, and sauerkraut on it. "Some breakfast," she muttered, feeling queasy.

"Want a bite?" He shoved it into her face.

"Ugh. You're not funny, Ronnie."

A short while later, they were back on the beach. A few hardy swimmers were in the water. A group of teenagers were hanging out in front of a tall, grassy dune. An elderly couple was walking a panting German shepherd along the water. Otherwise, the beach was empty.

"Hey, Mouse, want to go into town or something?" Ronnie suggested.

Instead of replying, Amy grabbed his arm.

"What's the matter?" he asked, startled by the fearful look on her face.

"Ronnie — look." She pointed to the beach house.

"Huh? What?" he asked, bewildered.

A wave of dread swept over Amy. Her breath caught in her throat.

"Amy, what is it?" Ronnie demanded.

"The beach house," she managed to say. "Look, Ronnie. There's someone in there."

12
Murder

A jagged streak of bright white lightning slanted over the ocean. A few seconds later, thunder rolled in like the tide.

Holding Ronnie's hand, Amy took a few cautious steps toward the beach house. "Did you see it? I saw a face in the window. *There.* See? There it is again."

"Yeah. I see," Ronnie said, picking up the pace to lead the way. "There's someone in there, all right."

"I'm . . . frightened," Amy admitted. "I mean — " She gasped and let go of Ronnie's hand as someone came out through the sliding-glass door and walked around the deck. "It's *Buddy*!" Amy exclaimed in a high-pitched squeak of a voice that revealed her shock.

"Whoa. I don't *believe* it!" Ronnie cried.

They stood frozen in place on the sand as Buddy

spotted them and came running across the beach, waving and calling. "Hey, guys! Guys!"

Another streak of jagged lightning burst high in the clouds, followed by the low rumble of thunder.

"Buddy — you're okay!" Amy cried. "We thought — "

"What happened? Where've you been?" Ronnie asked, slapping Buddy on the back.

"Hi," Buddy said shyly, pushing back his dark hair.

And then Amy and Ronnie both noticed the blood on the front of Buddy's white T-shirt. Still red. Still wet.

"Oh. Yeah." Buddy quickly realized what they were staring at. "I just cut myself." He held up a bandaged finger. "Making a sandwich. Do you believe how clumsy I am? I can't even slice bread."

"Buddy, where've you been?" Amy demanded, forcing her eyes away from the fresh bloodstain on the shirt. "We all thought you were . . . you know. Dead."

"I'm sorry," Buddy said, shifting his weight uncomfortably. "I went to my cousin's in Rockford. I mean, my mom took me there. I know I should've told you or something. But I was pretty messed up. I mean, after Maria died. I — "

"The police have been looking for you," Amy interrupted, studying his brown eyes, looking for the sadness there.

"I called them from my cousin's," Buddy said,

avoiding her hard stare. He started to walk. They followed beside him. "It . . . it was real hard to talk about it. But I told them everything. I mean, everything I knew. Which wasn't much."

"We were real worried," Ronnie said, patting Buddy's shoulder. "I mean, we felt *terrible*. No one told us you were alive."

"Really?" Buddy's face filled with surprise. "Someone should have told you. I called the police right away. I mean, as soon as I could talk without . . . as soon as I could talk."

"Well, what happened, Buddy?" Amy asked, stepping in front of him, forcing him to stop and face her. "What happened to Maria? Did she drown? When you two went swimming, did she — "

"We didn't," Buddy said, holding up a hand to stop her questions.

"You didn't go swimming?" Amy couldn't keep the shock from her voice.

Buddy looked away and cleared his throat. "It's still hard to talk about this, you know?"

"I'm sorry," Amy told him. "But we've all been so upset, so crazy. Every night, I dream that — "

"Maria went swimming, but I didn't," Buddy explained. "After you left, Amy, she and I tested the water. Maria wanted to swim. But I thought the undertow was too strong. It was pulling like crazy. I'm a real good swimmer, but I was afraid of it. So I decided not to go in."

He picked up a flat, gray pebble and heaved it

high in the air, his eyes following it as it landed back on the beach.

"And Maria?" Amy asked impatiently.

"She wanted to swim. I told her no. The water was too rough, too unpredictable. She called me a chicken. We sort of had an argument." His cheeks reddened. "You know how I get sometimes. I don't like to be called names."

"Was it a bad argument?" Amy asked.

Buddy shook his head. "No. It was short. I just said I wasn't going to swim, and she said she was going in without me. I said, fine, do whatever you want. I didn't really mean it, but I was angry. So I said good-bye and went into the house."

He stooped to pick up another stone, a smooth white oval. He swallowed hard a few times, then raised his eyes to Amy. "That was the last time I saw her."

Amy glanced at Ronnie to see if he believed Buddy's story. Ronnie's features were set in a grim frown. Then she turned back to Buddy, who was rolling the smooth rock around in his hand. "You really think she went swimming by herself?"

"Yeah. I think so. Out of stubbornness, probably." He heaved the stone to the ground. A loud sigh escaped his lips. "The next thing I knew, the police were all over the beach. When I heard they were searching for Maria, I realized what had happened. That she had . . . drowned."

He stooped down again and, unable to find a

stone, picked up a handful of sand. "I felt so guilty.
I guess I went a little crazy then," he said softly,
watching the sand as it sifted through his fingers.
"At least that's what my mom said. She said I wasn't
making any sense at all, just jabbering like a crazy
person. So she got me out of here and drove me to
my cousin's. It took me a couple of days before
. . . before I could *think* straight."

"I *still* can't think straight," Amy muttered.

Ronnie put a hand tenderly on her shoulder.

"I wasn't going to come back," Buddy said. "But
I decided you can't run away from things."

"Yeah, I guess," Ronnie said softly.

The sky grew even blacker, turning the rolling
ocean waters a dark olive shade. The wind picked
up, gusting and dipping around them, causing small
cyclones of sand to rise up off the beach.

"I didn't know Maria long," Buddy said, staring
at the water. "But I really cared about her."

Amy shivered. She buttoned the top button
of her dad's white shirt. "It's really getting
cold."

"Want to come in and warm up?" Buddy gestured
to the beach house. "I could make some hot choc-
olate or coffee."

"No. No thanks," Amy replied, glancing at Ronnie. "I want to get home. Thanks anyway, Buddy."

"I'm sure glad you're okay," Ronnie said, giving
Buddy another friendly slap on the shoulder.

"Yeah. Right. Thanks," Buddy replied. "Catch

you later." He turned and jogged back to the beach house.

Amy and Ronnie watched him disappear inside, the glass door sliding shut behind him. Then Amy looked up at Ronnie, her expression thoughtful, troubled. "Do you believe him?"

"Believe what? That he was at his cousin's? Yeah, I guess," Ronnie replied, rubbing his chin. "We *know* he got out of here in a hurry. When the police searched the beach house, it was empty."

"But do you believe the part about Maria deciding to go swimming by herself?"

"Well . . ." Ronnie shrugged.

"That doesn't sound like Maria at all," Amy said heatedly. "She was always very enthusiastic, always ready to do things. But she wasn't foolhardy or reckless."

"Yeah. You're right," Ronnie agreed. "But why would Buddy make up a lie? I mean — " He stopped, staring toward the shore.

Amy immediately saw what had caught his eye.

Something was huddled on the beach, just out of the swirling water.

Not something. Some*one*.

Someone lying facedown in the sand.

Running against the strong wind off the water, they arrived together. At first, they didn't recognize the boy, lying with his arms and legs sprawled across the sand, his face buried.

And then Amy cried, "Stuart!"

Puddles of dark blood had clotted on the back of

Stuart's head. His scalp had been smashed open, a slice of white skull showing through. Blood had soaked into his shirt and onto the sand around his head.

A few feet from his battered body lay a thick, driftwood log, bloodied at one end.

"He's been murdered," Ronnie said, holding Amy tightly, his hands suddenly as cold as death.

13
It's So Easy

Buddy pressed his forehead against the cool pane of the window as he stared out at the busy scene on the beach. Dark-uniformed policemen had formed a circle around the body down near the water. Other policemen spread over the beach and dunes, searching for clues.

A radio reporter stood outside the circle of policemen, trying to get his equipment to work. The local newspaper had sent two young reporters and a photographer to get the story.

Such a commotion, Buddy thought, unable to keep a satisfied smile from spreading across his face. The cool glass felt so good against his feverish forehead.

Such excitement.

He was excited, too, he had to admit.

Murder was so exciting.

And so easy.

All those movies and TV shows made it look hard, risky. TV murderers always had such remorse.

No one ever said how easy it is to kill someone.

Or how exciting.

He glanced up at the clearing sky. The storm had been a disappointment. A lot of noise and light, but little rain. It had passed over the beach in a matter of minutes, barely dampening the sand.

Barely washing away the blood.

The police had scurried to cover Stuart with a canvas tarp. But there was hardly any reason to bother, Buddy thought.

Now he watched them huddle around the tarp, talking among themselves, the fat photographer snapping away.

"Let's see you put me down now, Stuart," Buddy said aloud, pushing himself away from the window and starting to pace back and forth through the sparsely furnished living room. "Go ahead. Let's see you make fun of me now."

Stuart thought he was such a riot, Buddy told himself bitterly, pacing rapidly now, clasping his hands in front of him. He enjoyed giving me a hard time, making me look ridiculous.

They all did.

Well, Stuart had to pay.

Maria had to pay.

They'll *all* pay.

Sure, I'm an outsider, Buddy thought bitterly. Sure, I'm different from them. Maybe I don't belong in their crowd.

But they had no reason to laugh at me. To *lie* to me.

No one likes to be laughed at.

He stopped at the window and glanced down toward the shore. No one had moved.

No one's laughing now, Buddy thought happily.

An entire beach, and no one's laughing.

Off to the side, several yards from the circle of policemen, he saw Amy and Ronnie being questioned by two grim-faced policemen.

What's the matter, guys? Not laughing? Not spending your day laughing at Buddy for a change?

It was hard to decide which of them to kill first. He only knew that they both had to die.

And it was so easy. So *easy*.

Especially when you knew you could get away with it.

Humming "Earth Angel," a song he had just heard on the radio, Buddy changed into the clean T-shirt he had brought with him. He carefully packed the bloodied T-shirt into his backpack and hid the backpack in the big bedroom closet.

Then he hurried out to join Amy and Ronnie, fixing a shocked and horrified expression on his face as he ran.

High, white clouds still covered the sun, but the air had grown hot and humid. People clustered along the beach, gathering in small groups to talk and gossip about what had happened. Back near the dunes, a volleyball game was in progress, providing the only shouts and laughter that could be heard.

"I don't believe it," Buddy said to Amy and Ronnie. "Are there any suspects?"

Ronnie shook his head. Amy, her face pale and frightened, didn't look up.

"Any clues or anything?" Buddy asked, his face filled with concern.

"That's the murder weapon. Over there," Ronnie said, pointing to the driftwood log on the sand. The photographer was snapping shot after shot of it from every angle.

"Looks pretty heavy," Buddy said, staring at it.

"It's like a bad dream," Amy said to no one in particular. "First Maria. Now Stuart."

"Who are *you*?" a voice demanded.

Buddy turned to see one of the policemen who had been questioning Amy and Ronnie standing inches behind him. The police officer was wearing black uniform Bermuda shorts and a loose-fitting black, short-sleeved shirt with a silver badge pinned over the pocket. He had a slender, pale face dotted with pimples, topped with a close-cropped blond crewcut. His eyes were tiny, gray, and intense.

Buddy told the officer his name. "My mom and I are staying at the beach house." He pointed.

"Where's your mom?" the policeman asked curtly, his tiny eyes locked on Buddy's.

"In town, I think. She isn't home."

"You knew Stuart Miller?" The policeman's eyes continued to accuse Buddy.

Buddy stared right back at him. "I just met him about a week ago. I guess you'd say we were kind of friends."

"Did you see him this morning?"

Buddy shook his head. "No."

A team of white-uniformed medics had arrived and were struggling to load Stuart's body onto a canvas stretcher. As they tried to lift the stretcher, one side dipped, and the body rolled off, giving everyone a view of Stuart's bashed-in skull.

"Did you see anything at all from the beach house?" the policeman asked, keeping his voice low and professional.

"No," Buddy told him. "I just got back a few minutes ago. I was away."

Amy jerked her head up, suddenly remembering something about Buddy. The bloody shirt. The bloodstain that was splattered over the front of it.

"I was at my cousin's in Rockford. I haven't even unpacked yet," Buddy was telling the policeman.

But you unpacked a clean shirt, Amy thought, staring hard at Buddy.

Could all that blood have really come from a cut finger?

She studied his face as he answered the policeman's questions. But it revealed nothing to her.

You have no reason to suspect Buddy, she scolded herself. Buddy is as upset as you are.

He's just another teenager. He isn't a murderer.

Staring at him, Amy suddenly saw a different picture of him. She suddenly saw him stranded in

the water, calling frantically to them. And she saw
Ronnie and Stuart running across the beach, waving
Buddy's swim trunks.

Once again, Amy saw the distressed look on Buddy's face. She saw him floundering about, trying to
keep afloat on the incoming waves, shouting to
them, begging them for his trunks.

It was all so funny.

It was all so much fun.

Hard to believe it was only about a week ago.

Funny how the mind jumps around, Amy
thought. When there's a tragedy, when something
truly horrifying happens, the mind wants to leap
away to happier times, to brighter pictures.

She pictured poor, frantic Buddy, bobbing
around helplessly, stranded in the ocean and, without realizing it, started to laugh.

"What's so funny?" Buddy asked sternly, cutting
into her thoughts.

"Nothing," Amy replied quickly — and felt a
stab of fear.

Buddy had the strangest, angriest expression on
his face.

14
Running From Buddy

"Rotate! Rotate!"

The girl with short blonde hair, a dazzling emerald-green swimsuit, and a figure like Jayne Mansfield's, cupped her hands over her mouth as she shouted. The other team members obediently changed position.

"Your serve!" the girl called to Amy, heaving the volleyball at her.

Amy caught the ball against her chest. It nearly knocked her breath away. Why did that girl have to throw so hard? And why was she always yelling "Rotate!" at the top of her lungs?

"Serve it over the net, Mouse," Ronnie called to her from his position at the net.

"Very helpful advice," Amy replied, rolling her eyes.

Some kids laughed.

Amy didn't think it was funny. The net looked

so high. She held the ball up in her tiny palm and poised her other hand to hit it.

If only I were six inches taller, she thought, this game would be more fun.

Clouds drifted over the sun, immediately cooling the air. The forecast called for more rain. It had rained every single day this week.

Such a gloomy vacation.

"Serve it — don't study it!" a boy on the other team yelled. Also very helpful.

Amy slugged the ball with all her might. She cried out, watching it sail right into the net.

"Net ball!" the girl in the emerald swimsuit yelled.

A picture flashed into Amy's mind of serving the ball right into that girl's teeth.

"Do over!"

Ronnie retrieved the ball from the sand and tossed it back to Amy. "Over the net! Over the net!" he called.

"What's the score?" someone yelled.

"Hey look —" someone else shouted. Everyone turned to the water to see a boy water-skiing behind a roaring powerboat, very close to shore.

They clapped and cheered when the skier toppled over almost immediately, disappearing in a tall splash of white froth.

The sky darkened. Four sea gulls glided overhead, slender white Vs against the charcoal sky.

Amy positioned herself to serve again. She raised

the ball and tightened her other fist, preparing to hit it.

The net loomed over her, ruffling slightly in the quickening breeze.

Everyone is watching me, she thought, concentrating, staring at the ball, then raising her eyes to the net.

Over. Over. Over. *Please* go over.

She hit it solidly. It rose higher this time, but skimmed the net as it went over.

There were sighs and groans from her teammates. She glanced to the side to see Ronnie shaking his head.

Hey, guys, it's only a game, Amy thought bitterly.

"Your serve!" the girl in the emerald suit called to the other side.

"Rotate! Rotate!" came the cry over there.

"What's the score?" a girl called.

"It's sixteen to three. A tie!" some joker replied.

"Look alive, gang!" the girl in the emerald suit instructed, hands on her knees, eyes on the ball.

Who made *her* captain? Amy wondered.

Ronnie grinned at her. She stuck her tongue out at him.

These kids sure take their volleyball seriously, she thought, studying their intense expressions as the serve flew over the net and everyone sprung into action, jumping high, arms flying, hands slapping.

The ball swooped in front of her. She dived toward it, bringing her hands up fast.

Success!

The ball sailed over the net and bounced on the sand.

Grinning happily, Amy picked herself up from the ground, brushing off her pink short-shorts.

"Good hit!" the girl in the emerald suit called, giving her a thumbs-up.

"Thanks!" Amy cried. "What's your name?"

"Amy," the girl called.

Amy's mouth dropped open in surprise. "Me, too!" she yelled.

"Hi, Amy," the girl said, laughing.

"Hi, Amy!"

This was fun. Amy and Ronnie didn't know these kids. None of them were from Ridgefield. But they seemed like a nice bunch of kids, all very enthusiastic and very athletic.

It's great to lose yourself in a game, to concentrate on having fun, Amy thought, watching the next server get into position.

But she couldn't help it. She couldn't concentrate entirely. She couldn't control her mind. She found her thoughts wandering to Maria.

She couldn't stop thinking about her.

Every time a girl with a long, dark ponytail walked by on the beach, Amy was ready to call, "Maria!"

Buddy also hovered in her thoughts.

The blood on his T-shirt.

The strange, angry expression on his face as he had stared at her that afternoon.

It had frightened her so much.

It still frightened her.

She had no reason to believe that Buddy was a liar. But his story about Maria wanting to swim in a dangerous undertow — swim all by herself, even though she wasn't a strong swimmer — it didn't make sense.

It didn't ring true.

Maria wouldn't have swum very far out by herself. She would've stayed close to shore.

And if she had stayed close to shore, if she had drowned close to shore, her body would have washed up on the beach by now.

Her body.

Ugh.

Amy couldn't stop these dreadful, frightening thoughts.

No matter how hard Amy tried to push her to the back of her mind, Maria was always there. Maria and Buddy.

The bloody T-shirt.

Stuart's battered, bloody head.

"Look out!" someone yelled.

The ball hit her on the shoulder, bounced up. She slapped at it, kept it alive. And the girl beside her slapped it over the net for a point.

Amy joined in the jubilant cheering by her teammates

This is fun, she repeated to herself. I am entitled to have a little fun this summer.

She was sorry when the game ended. Twenty-one to fourteen.

"I think we were just warming up," Ronnie said, walking over to her, the front of his navy blue, sleeveless T-shirt darkened with a circle of sweat.

"I've got to practice my serve," Amy said, smiling.

"We'll get you a stool to stand on, Mouse."

"Har de har har," Amy said sarcastically, imitating the TV comedian Jackie Gleason. "That's rich. That's really rich! You're cruisin' for a bruisin', Ronnie."

He dropped to his knees to search through his beach bag. Pulling out his wristwatch, his eyes went wide with alarm. "Oh, my gosh! I promised my parents I'd come home early and help. They're having a big barbecue tonight. About twenty people."

Amy glanced up at the darkening sky. Black clouds were rolling rapidly over the beach. "Looks like it might be rained out," she said, buttoning her dad's white shirt she always used as a beach wrap.

"Oh, great," Ronnie muttered, rolling his eyes. "Twenty people crammed into our tiny cottage. Dad out barbecuing in the rain. Sounds like a great evening."

"Have fun," Amy said wistfully.

"I've got to run," Ronnie said, zipping up the beach bag and climbing to his feet. "You coming?"

"No. Think I'll stay and watch the clouds for a

bit," Amy said. "I love this kind of weather. So cool and wet. So dramatic."

He waved a quick good-bye and, carrying his sandals, ran full speed over the sand toward the road.

Amy watched him for a while, thinking of how he resembled a long, lanky giraffe when he ran. Then she turned back to the beach.

A few minutes before, it had been crowded with swimmers and sunbathers. But the threatening clouds had nearly emptied the beach. Carrying their beach chairs, umbrellas, coolers, and blankets, people were making their way over the low dunes to the road, eager to get home before the rains came.

Wrapping her arms around her chest against the chill air, Amy wandered down to the water. The cold, wet wind felt so refreshing blowing through her hair. Wine-colored waves washed noisily to shore. She walked in up to her ankles. The water felt surprisingly warm.

The beach was deserted now, except for two elderly fishermen far off at one end, standing patiently, poles in the water, and a cluster of teenaged boys up by the dunes, dressed mostly in blue denim, sneaking cigarettes, laughing boisterously.

Amy walked for a while, letting the warm, frothy water wash over her bare feet. She had finally decided to return home when, out of the corner of her eye, she saw someone running toward her at full speed.

She squinted against the glare, watching him

grow larger as he approached. Who would be running to her with such urgency?

"Buddy!" she cried his name aloud as his face came into clear view.

And felt the alarm race through her body.

Such heavy dread.

Buddy. Running after her.

Before she even realized what she was doing, Amy splashed out of the water and, her heart pounding, her dread weighing her down, began to run from him.

Her bare feet sank into the soft wet sand.

She felt as if she were running uphill.

She glanced back to see him pick up speed, his arms outstretched, his face bright red. He was shouting something, calling to her, but the roar of the wind drowned out all other sound.

She was running fast now, as fast as she could.

Trying to outrun the dread. Trying to outrun her sudden burst of fear.

But he was right behind her now.

She uttered a silent cry as his arms circled her waist and he tackled her to the sand.

15
Amy's Big Decision

Crying out in protest, Amy pulled out of his grasp and struggled to her feet.

To her surprise, Buddy remained on his stomach, laughing, reaching for her playfully. Her chest heaving, gasping to catch her breath, Amy stood tensely poised, trying to decide whether to stay or run.

His laughter made her hesitate.

"Amy, you're pretty fast!" he exclaimed, climbing to his knees.

Waiting for her heart to stop racing, she eyed him warily.

"Why'd you run?" he asked, not standing up. "Didn't you see that it was me?"

His dark hair, normally neatly brushed, was in disarray. The front of his T-shirt was covered with wet sand.

"I — I don't know," Amy replied, starting to feel a little calmer. "You scared me," she added.

Why *did* she run? she asked herself.

Why *was* she so filled with dread at the sight of him, so filled with *terror*?

"Sorry," he said, finally climbing to his feet, brushing himself off with both hands. He walked close to her, close enough that she could smell his sweat. He was more than a head taller than she, and so broad and muscular.

He was usually so awkward, so shy, that she'd never realized how powerfully built he was, how solid.

"I didn't mean to scare you," he said, his expression turning serious. "I was just running to catch up to you."

"I . . . I was just going home," she said, avoiding his dark eyes.

"I thought maybe we could talk or something," he said, disappointed.

"No. I think I have to go," Amy replied, realizing that they were the only ones on the beach. Even the two fishermen had disappeared from view.

"It's just that . . . well, I've been feeling really sad," Buddy said shyly, lowering his eyes to the sand.

"I'm sorry," Amy said. She fiddled nervously with the shirt flaps that came down below the legs of her short-shorts.

"I've been kind of lonely, I guess," Buddy continued. "I mean, I've had a lot of time to think. And I can't stop thinking about things. You know."

Amy eyed him silently, surprised at his honesty,

surprised that he felt close enough to her to confide in her like this.

"I've had such terrible dreams about Maria," he blurted out. He sighed, as if he were relieved that he'd managed to say it.

"Me, too," Amy said quietly.

"I wanted someone to talk to," Buddy said, turning his eyes to hers. "Someone who knew Maria."

Maybe I've misjudged him, Amy thought.

He seems so sad, so broken up.

He's being so honest with me. And here I've been, imagining such dreadful things about him. Accusing him of being a murderer.

The wind gusted, carried a sting. Black clouds hovered low.

None of us were fair to Buddy, Amy thought, studying him. He was an outsider, and we never really gave him a chance.

"I wondered . . ." he started. "Could we take a short walk, just to my house? We could talk on the way." He trained his eyes on her, pleading eyes, his expression hopeful.

"Well . . ." she glanced up at the lowering sky. "It's going to storm, I think."

"Just a short walk," he pleaded. "If it starts to rain, you can come inside and wait it out."

"Well . . ."

"Come on," he urged, a smile slowly forming on his handsome face. "I won't bite. Promise."

Amy gazed into his eyes, so dark and sad.

Then she glanced over his shoulder. In the near

distance, at the spot where the beach curved away, the beach house loomed darkly in the water. The incoming tide lapped at its fragile stilts.

Should I go with him? Amy wondered.

She realized that her heart was still racing. Her mouth felt as dry as sand.

Such uncertainty.

Should I go to the beach house with him?

He stood watching her, hands at his sides, patiently waiting for her to decide.

PART FOUR

This Summer

16
A Discovery
in the Beach House

"I keep thinking we'll run into Lucy and Kip," Ashley said, her eyes scanning the crowded beach.

It was a hot, humid day, the sun high in a hazy gray sky, no breeze at all, even near the ocean. The waves were low and far apart, breaking right on the shore. Ashley noticed that the ocean was nearly as crowded as the beach, filled with people trying to cool off.

She and Ross made their way past tilted beach umbrellas and sleeping sunbathers and headed toward the water.

Nearby, two tall young black men in baggy Hammer pants were practicing a complicated dance step, their bare feet sinking into the sand, their boom box blaring.

"It's so noisy today," Ross complained.

"You're starting to sound like an old man," Ashley teased. She did an imitation of a grouchy old geezer: *"Turn that radio down! Are you deaf or something?"*

He frowned. "I don't sound like that," he protested, giving her shoulder a playful shove, nearly sending her sprawling into two young women sunbathing on a blanket with their halter tops off.

"If it's too loud, you're too old!" Ashley declared. She cried out suddenly, grabbed his arm, then quickly released it.

"Sorry," she said, shutting her eyes for a moment. "I thought I saw Lucy. This keeps happening to me." She reopened them and pointed. "That girl over there. Doesn't she look just like her?"

Ross tried to follow her gaze. "Sorry. I don't see her."

"She just sat down," Ashley said. "Never mind."

They walked on a little farther, the cry of children's voices in their ears. A boy of ten or eleven, running with his yellow boogie board in his hands, ran right into Ross.

"Whoa!" Ross staggered backward.

"Sorry!" the boy called, and kept right on running.

"Spring a leak!" Ross shouted after him.

Ashley laughed. "Boogie boards can't spring leaks, you dork."

"I *know* that," Ross said edgily, his eyes on a tall, extremely well-built girl in a chartreuse string bikini.

After the girl disappeared behind a beach umbrella, he turned back to Ashley. "I keep thinking

I see Kip and Lucy, too," he said quietly. "I mean, they've got to be somewhere — right?"

"Yeah," Ashley agreed, taking his arm. "Yuck. You're sweaty."

"What do you expect? It's really hot, isn't it?" he said defensively. He glanced up to the sky as a large, dark cloud rolled over the sun, sending a wide shadow rolling over the beach. "Maybe it'll rain and cool things off."

"Two people can't just disappear into thin air," Ashley said, sighing, lost in her own troubled thoughts.

"It's so weird," Ross agreed, shaking his head. "It's been days. No sign of them. Not a clue."

"The police tried to make Lucy's parents believe that she and Kip had run away together," Ashley said. "Do you believe that? I mean, Lucy wasn't that serious about Kip. I don't even think she liked him that much."

"I don't know," Ross said thoughtfully. "It's not nice to say. I mean, since he's missing and everything. But I didn't like him much, either. I thought he was a creep."

"Kip had such a chip on his shoulder," Ashley agreed. "He really thought we looked down on him just because he was a townie and had to have a summer job."

"I tried to be friendly to him," Ross said, readjusting his ponytail as they walked. "But he'd just turn away. You know. Turn his back and take a nap or something."

"And he had no sense of humor at all," Ashley added. "Joking around actually made him angry."

"I can't believe we're talking about Kip as if he's dead," Ross said, swallowing hard.

"Yeah. If Kip is dead, it means that Lucy . . ." Ashley didn't want to finish her sentence.

"I kept thinking maybe they were kidnapped," Ross said, staring out at the ocean, olive green under the darkening sky.

"But why would anyone kidnap *them*?" Ashley asked. "Lucy's dad is a travel agent, and her mom's a secretary. They don't have any money. Besides, if it was a kidnapping, the kidnappers would have called by now."

"Well, if it's not a kidnapping, what is it?" Ross cried heatedly. "Where *are* they?"

"Let's change the subject," Ashley said, resting a hand on his shoulder. "We've been over this again and again. It's not getting us anywhere. It's only making us feel worse."

"Yeah, I know," he replied glumly.

Ashley slipped off her blue and white rubber Nike flip-flops and, carrying them, went wading into the water. "Ooh — I thought it'd be warmer!"

Ross walked with her, staying up on dry sand.

"So are we going to Brad's or not?" Ashley asked, speaking reluctantly, not eager to bring up what she knew was a sore subject.

"We?" Ross asked sarcastically. "You mean your new boyfriend asked *me* to come along, too?"

"Stop it, Ross," Ashley scolded, holding her temper. "He's not my new boyfriend. Don't be a jerk. And you *know* he invited both of us — not just me — to come play tennis."

"Who needs him?" Ross said bitterly.

"I just think it'd be fun, that's all. Brad says his clay court is fabulous. And it's his. It's private. You've been complaining about having to wait every morning at the public courts."

"I know, but — "

"And you've been complaining about how terrible the courts are. The bad nets. The holes in the asphalt."

"I know," Ross said petulantly. He picked up a handful of sand and tossed it back down.

"Brad seems like a really nice guy," Ashley continued. "Aren't you at all curious about his house? I mean, you know the houses along Ocean Drive. They're enormous! They're not houses — they're estates! We could pretend we're fabulously wealthy for a day."

"You want to be fabulously wealthy with Brad," Ross accused. "Admit it. You don't want me tagging along."

"Aaaagh!" Ashley uttered an exasperated cry. "Don't start that, Ross! I'm warning you!" She kicked angrily at the water, trying to splash him.

"Yeah, yeah. We've been over all this before, too," Ross grumbled, dodging away from the spray of water, making a disgusted face.

"I guess we've been over *everything* before," Ashley said, feeling her anger rise, unable to hold it down any longer. "I guess maybe we've said it all. We're bored with each other, huh?"

"I didn't say that," he quickly insisted, his dark eyes lighting up. "You're just trying to pick a fight, Ashley, so you can go out with Brad with a clean conscience."

Ashley groaned angrily. She ran out of the water, eager to confront him. "I warned you — "

His eyes went wide with surprise, and he raised his hands in a sign of truce. "Okay, okay." His hands still raised, he tried to back away from her, but stumbled over a large crab shell and fell over backwards, landing jarringly hard on the sand.

Ashley couldn't help it. She wanted to stay angry. But he looked so ridiculous, she started to laugh.

"What's so funny?" he demanded, reddening, still sprawled in the sand.

"You looked like a big crab yourself," Ashley teased.

He scowled.

She knew he hated to be teased. But she *wanted* to make him angry. He deserved it.

"Better watch out," he said, his expression softening a little. "Crabs like to pinch."

She laughed and reached out to help him up. But he grabbed her hands and, with a hard tug, pulled her down on top of him.

"Ross, stop it!" she scolded, trying to free herself. "It's too crowded here. It — "

His arms had slipped around her waist, and he

was reaching his head up to kiss her. She decided
not to resist. They kissed, long and hard.

"Get up!" he groaned as she pulled her face away
from his. "You're *crushing* me!"

"Okay. Don't be insulting."

As she started to lift herself off him, the rain
started, a sudden downpour, enormous raindrops
pounding the beach, drumming the sand like thunder.

In seconds, the sound of the rain was drowned
out by the shouts and squeals of swimmers and sunbathers, who were frantically gathering up their
coolers, blankets, and equipment and making a mad
dash for cover.

Ashley leapt to her feet and pulled Ross up. "It's
freezing cold!" she shrieked as the large raindrops
pelted her skin.

Ross laughed. "I told you the rain would cool
things off!"

She grabbed his hand and began pulling him away
from the ocean. "I'm freezing. We've got to find a
place to — "

Her hair was already sopping wet, flattened
against her head. Sheets of rain hammered down,
making it hard to see.

"Where are you pulling me?" Ross shouted over
the rain.

"I don't know. I'm just — " And then the beach
house came into view.

Without even thinking about it, she began pulling
him toward it. He saw it, too, and they both began

to run. The rain stung their shoulders. Shivering from the cold, they made their way, running as fast as they could, stumbling blindly toward the beach house.

Ross reached it first, raced up onto the deck, and ran around to the sliding-glass door in front, pulling it open. A few seconds later they were huddled together in the living room, soaked through and through, staring out at the sheets of rain through the glass door at the long stretch of beach, now all shades of gray, completely deserted.

"I — I'm freezing," Ashley said through chattering teeth, wrapping her wet arms around her bare skin. Her string bikini didn't provide much warmth. "Lend me your T-shirt."

Ross was shivering, too. "Are you kidding? It's totally soaked. It wouldn't warm you up."

"Maybe there are some towels in this house," Ashley suggested in desperation. "Or a robe or something."

Ross hopped up and down, forcing some of the water off. "In a deserted beach house that's been empty for thirty years?"

She made a disgusted face. "It's worth a try. Let's look."

Without waiting for him to reply, she headed for the hallway. Rain drummed on the roof and spattered the windows. The steady wash of the ocean waves competed with the pounding of the rain.

There were no towels in the small bathroom. Leaving a trail of water, she hurried into the first bedroom. It was unfurnished except for a dresser and a wooden double bed with a bare mattress. Frantically, she pulled out the dresser drawers. Empty.

With an unhappy groan, she made her way to the closet and slid open the door. It was dark inside. She peered in. It appeared to be empty.

She stepped inside.

Wow, she thought. She stuck her head out and called to Ross. "Hey, Ross. Ross! Come look at this closet. It's enormous!"

"What?" he called, sounding very far away. He must still be in the living room, she realized. But she could barely hear him over the sound of the rain.

"Come see this closet!" she repeated, screaming from the closet doorway.

"No, thanks," she heard him call back to her. "I'm not real interested in closets. Did you find any towels?"

"No," she replied, discouraged.

It's so dark in here, she thought. This closet seems bigger than the bedroom!

Shivering, she started to make her way out when her foot touched something.

Something soft that clung to her foot.

Gasping for breath, Ashley kicked at it, but it wouldn't let go.

And then she started to scream.

17
Trouble for Ross

"Ashley — what? Where are you?"

Ross burst into the open closet, his voice filled with alarm. "Are you okay?"

"Yes. Sorry," she said, her voice still quavering. "There was something on the floor. I — I picked it up. It's — "

She put a hand on his chest and gave him a soft push, then followed him out of the dark closet.

In the gray light from the bedroom window she examined what she had found.

"It's just a scarf," Ross said.

Her eyes wide with surprise, Ashley didn't reply.

"Ashley, it's just a scarf," Ross repeated impatiently. "What's the big deal?"

"It's Lucy's," Ashley finally managed to say, still staring at it in horror. She ran the green, silky scarf through her trembling fingers. "It's the fancy silk scarf I gave Lucy for her last birthday."

"How did it get in the closet?" Ross asked.

Ashley stared at the scarf, then raised her eyes to his. "I don't know."

Behind the tall, perfectly trimmed hedges that shielded it from the road, Brad's summer house rose up like a castle. Three stories tall, it hovered over a wide, manicured lawn, an enormous pink-gray stone structure, rows of tall windows reflecting the sun, each window framed by white shutters.

Ashley pulled her parents' station wagon up the seemingly endless driveway, past a flower garden the size of a meadow, and parked in the circle in front of the four-car garage.

"Is this a house or a hotel?" Ross asked, wide-eyed as they made their way along the curving flagstone walk.

"Brad wasn't kidding when he said he was rich," Ashley said, admiring a delicate brass sculpture of a ballerina surrounded by a sea of bright orange and yellow tiger lilies.

"I can't believe just one family lives in this house," Ross said, shaking his head. "I mean, there are so many rooms — how do they find each other?"

"Which is the front door?" Ashley asked, swinging her tennis racket onto her shoulder. From their vantage point on the front walk, there appeared to be three different doors that could be the front door.

"Let's just get out of here," Ross said.

Ashley stared at him, trying to decide if he was serious. He was.

"We don't belong here," Ross said, tugging at

his short ponytail nervously. "We don't *like* tea and crumpets."

Ashley laughed. "We're here to play tennis, remember? Just because the house is kind of big doesn't mean they serve tea and cumpets."

"What *is* a crumpet, anyway?" Ross asked fretfully. "I don't even know what one is."

"Well, I'm not leaving just because you don't know what a crumpet is," Ashley insisted. "Did you bring a bathing suit? Brad has a pool, too."

"I know." Ross rolled his eyes. "Brad has everything."

"Don't start," Ashley warned. They stopped in front of the first door, freshly painted white like the shutters, a polished brass door knocker in the middle. "Let's try this door."

Ashley looked for a doorbell. Not finding one, she reached for the brass door knocker.

She had just started to pull it back when the door swung open. "Oh!" Ashley cried, startled.

A stern-faced servant in a starched white uniform stared out at them. She was a thin, middle-aged woman with dramatic, dark eyes ringed by dark circles. She had short, bushy hair that must have once been black but was now streaked with wide stripes of gray. "Won't you come in?" she asked coldly, motioning for them to enter.

Ashley stepped into the front entranceway. Despite the July heat, the servant's uniform was long-sleeved, and the starched white collar of her blouse came up high on her neck.

"Brad is expecting you," she said, staring at them with her dark eyes, looking them up and down as if inspecting for fleas.

At that moment, Brad entered the room, dressed in tennis whites, carrying a racket. He was followed by the tall red-haired girl Ashley had seen with him at the beach.

"Your guests have arrived," the servant announced. She turned and walked quickly from the room, her white, rubber-soled shoes squeaking across the parquet floor.

"Hi, how's it going?" Brad called cheerfully, twirling the tennis racket, his eyes on Ashley. "Don't pay any attention to Mary. She's a bit weird."

"She kept staring at us," Ashley whispered, not certain whether the servant was still in hearing range.

"Probably just nearsighted," Brad said. He gestured to the tall girl beside him. "Have you met my cousin Sharon? Sharon, this is Ashley and Ross."

She's his cousin, Ashley thought, finding herself somewhat relieved. Everyone said hello. Ross stepped forward awkwardly to shake hands with Sharon. "Nice little cottage you have here," he told Brad. He tried to make it sound light, but it came out sarcastic.

"It's a perfect day for tennis," Brad said, smiling at Ashley. "Let me see your racket." He took it from her, unzipped the cover, and examined it as he led them through the house. "Excellent. This is excellent. I used to have one like this."

Ashley tried to see the house as they followed the wide hallway to the back. There were so many rooms. She saw at least two sitting rooms, elegantly furnished in heavy-looking, country-style antiques. They passed an enormous library, and a dining room with an endless oak table, set for at least sixteen people, a centerpiece of purple and white orchids decorating the center.

Mary, the servant, stood stiffly in the kitchen as they passed. She held a large silver tray stacked high with white dinner plates. She stared at them, her expression rigid, standing in a rectangle of sunlight from the kitchen window, her white uniform appearing to shimmer in the light.

The back yard rolled smoothly like a green carpet. Beyond another garden stood the pool house. Beyond it stood the Olympic-sized pool. A long, two-story guest house stood to the far right, and just beyond that was the red clay tennis court. In the distance, the grass gave way to sand where the dunes began, leading to the ocean.

"Wow! The ocean in your back yard!" Ashley exclaimed, her eyes trying to take in everything.

"Yeah. At night, I can hear it up in my room. It's like having one of those wave-sound machines," Brad said.

Ashley was suddenly aware that Sharon hadn't said a word. She turned to see Sharon staring at her thoughtfully. Wonder what *her* problem is? Ashley thought uncomfortably. And then decided that maybe Sharon was just shy.

"Any sign of Kip and Lucy?" Brad asked suddenly, the smile fading as his expression turned serious. He pulled the cover off his tennis racket. "Have they been found?"

"No," Ashley replied quietly. "No word about them. The police think they ran off together, but I don't believe it."

"Why not?" Sharon asked, her first words since they'd met. She had a husky, deep voice, low and sexy.

"Lucy isn't the type," Ashley replied. "I've known her forever. She wouldn't just run away." She turned to Brad. "I found a scarf of Lucy's. In the beach house."

His eyes widened in surprise. "The beach house?"

"You know. The empty house at the end of the beach."

"How did it get *there*?" Brad asked, shielding his eyes from the bright afternoon sunlight.

"Well, she and Kip used to go there to make out," Ashley said. "I found the scarf on the floor of a bedroom closet."

"But there was no sign of violence?" Brad asked, his eyes burning into hers.

Ashley shook her head. "No sign of anything. Just the scarf on the closet floor."

"Weird," Sharon said.

Brad didn't say anything. "Let's play doubles,"

he suggested, changing the subject. "Ashley and I will play you two."

Ashley saw a brief look of objection form on Ross's face, but he didn't say anything. Carrying his racket in both hands, he followed Sharon across the smooth court.

"Let's warm up a bit first," Ross said, adjusting his sunglasses as he positioned himself near the net. "I'm not used to a soft court like this."

"You'll like it," Sharon assured him. "It's a whole different sport." She arched her long body as she served, and the ball sailed easily over the net.

They warmed up, hitting the ball easily back and forth. To Ashley's surprise, Brad wasn't a very good tennis player. He moved awkwardly, uncertainly, and his swing was unpredictable, often wild.

Despite his lack of athletic prowess, she found herself drawn to him. He was really nice looking and seemed easygoing and modest, comfortable with being so rich, but not the least bit stuck-up because of it.

As they played, she could feel Brad's eyes on her. Whenever she turned to him, he flashed her his warmest smile.

He likes me, too, she realized.

In his shy way, he's coming on to me.

They played a complete set, pausing only when Mary brought out a tray of lemonade and iced tea. By the time they had finished — with Sharon and Ross winning the last two games and the set — the sun was lowering itself behind the house.

"How about a swim?" Brad asked Ashley, handing her a white towel to wipe the perspiration off her forehead.

"Well . . ." Ashley turned her eyes to Ross. He was glaring at her angrily.

He's obviously picked up the vibes between Brad and me, Ashley thought with dread.

Brad *had* been pretty obvious about it, talking only to Ashley, staring at her, smiling at her all afternoon.

Please, Ross, thought Ashley, staring at him meaningfully. Please don't lose your temper. Please don't make a fool of yourself. Please don't embarrass me in front of Brad and Sharon.

"I'd love to come back and swim sometime," Ashley told Brad. "But it's getting late."

"Okay. How about tomorrow?" Brad asked with obvious eagerness.

Ashley could see the annoyance spreading on Ross's face.

I'm so tired of his constant jealousy, of his stupid possessiveness, Ashley thought. I'm sick of it. Sick. "That would be great," she told Brad, avoiding Ross's eyes.

"One thing I wanted to show you," Brad said, putting the tennis racket back in Ashley's hand. "About your follow-through. I noticed this while we were playing."

He stepped behind her and put his arms around her, grabbing her wrists. "Now, I noticed when you swing . . ."

It was obvious to Ashley that Brad just wanted to put his arms around her. It was a clumsy trick, she thought.

But sweet.

Ross must not have agreed. Ashley looked up to see him heave his racket angrily to the ground. "Bye, Ashley," he muttered through gritted teeth.

"Hey, Ross — " Ashley started.

But Ross took off, jogging angrily toward the house.

"Hey!" Mary cried out. The servant was on her way to collect the drink tray, and Ross nearly barreled right into her. Her face turned scarlet as she dodged out of the way.

Ross called, "Sorry," and kept running.

"Ross, come back!" Ashley pulled out of Brad's grip and took a few steps toward Ross. "Come on, Ross! Brad was just showing me — "

Ross disappeared around the side of the house.

"Oh, let him go," Ashley said, exasperated.

"Hey, what's his problem?" Brad said, putting a hand on her shoulder. "I didn't mean anything."

Ashley sighed, staring at the house. "He's impossible. Really."

"What a short fuse," Sharon said, helping Mary pick up the heavy silver tray.

"Let him go," Ashley repeated.

This was the last straw. Ross had no right to storm off like that — and no right to embarrass her in front of Brad and Sharon.

No right at all.

I've had it with him, she told herself. And this time, I mean it.

She smiled at Brad. "How about that swim?"

She didn't hear from Ross that night.

The next afternoon, an afternoon of high clouds in a hazy, yellow sky, she was shopping in town, digging through the pile of bathing suits on the sale table at the Dunehampton Shop. She didn't see anything she liked. Everything had been picked over this late in the season.

Stepping out of the small shop, she decided to look in the bookstore across the street for something for her brothers. She was about to cross the narrow street when a hand grabbed her shoulder.

"Ross!"

His features were taut, his eyes locked onto hers. "I want to talk to you."

"No!" she cried, and pulled free. She started to cross, but the street was filled with cars, moving quickly.

"Come back!" he ordered.

The sidewalk was crowded. It wasn't much of a beach day, so everyone had jammed into town to stroll and window-shop.

"Go away, Ross. I mean it," Ashley said coldly.

"Ashley, I want to apologize," he said, reaching for her arm again.

"Ross, I'm sorry," she said heatedly, embarrassed that people were watching them, eaves-dropping on them as they waited to cross the street. "I really don't want to hear it."

"But I want to *apologize*," he insisted, his voice tightening in a whine. Others started to cross, but he held her back.

"Go away, Ross," she said in a low voice, trying to keep calm.

"But, Ashley — "

Suddenly, a large figure loomed in front of them. "Let go of her, man," Denny said. He raised both of his big hands and shoved Ross into the curb.

"Whoa — " Ross shouted, reddening with anger.

"The girl doesn't want to talk to you, man," Denny said menacingly, glancing at Ashley, then giving Ross another hard shove.

"Don't touch me, man," Ross cried angrily, slapping at Denny's arms, lashing out with both hands. Despite his anger, his face filled with fear. Denny was bigger. And stronger. And meaner.

"I warned you," Denny flared angrily.

"Denny — stop! Please!" Ashley screamed. "Denny — what are you going to *do*?"

18
A Word From the Dead

"Back off!" Ross yelled to Denny. "I mean it — back off!"

Behind Ashley, people were shouting in alarm. Ashley covered her ears with both hands. "Denny, *please!*" she screamed.

She tried to grab Denny's shoulder and hold him back. But he was so big, and moving so quickly now, she bounced right off him.

She regained her balance and turned her eyes back to the street in time to see Denny drive his fist into Ross's stomach.

To Ashley's horror, it all seemed to go into slow motion. She saw Ross's eyes bulge with surprise. Then his mouth burst open in a hideous groan. Denny's fist pulled back. Denny leaned away.

Ross's hands flailed in the air helplessly. His eyes rolled up in his head.

Another groan, this one silent.

And Ross toppled to his knees. His head went

137

down, and he dropped onto all fours and began to retch onto the curb.

Loud, excited voices surrounded Ashley, grew louder, even though her hands still sheltered her ears.

And then two black-uniformed town police officers came hurtling across the street.

"Later," Denny said to her, a strange, pleased smile on his face. And he darted into the crowd of onlookers and disappeared.

This isn't happening, Ashley thought, staring down at the retching figure on his hands and knees in the street.

This can't be happening.

The two policemen were trying to pull Ross to his feet, each one lifting a shoulder. Ross was breathing a little steadier now, one hand still holding his stomach.

Without even realizing that she was fleeing, Ashley backed into the crowd. She turned and saw Denny making his way down the block, swinging both of his powerful arms as he hurried away.

Denny's dangerous, Ashley decided. I used to think he was just a big clown.

But he's dangerous.

And he seems to have a thing about me.

A wave of fear swept over her. She pushed her way through the crowd and headed for home.

That night when she was getting ready for bed, Ross called. Ashley chased her brother from the room and sat down on the edge of her bed, holding the cordless phone, trying to decide how to talk to him.

She felt bad about that afternoon.

But she had made up her mind about Ross.

All afternoon, she had walked by herself on the beach. Starting at the low, grassy dunes, she had walked to the beach house and back, staring out at the rolling, tossing water, staring at the sea gulls soaring and diving, riding on the surface, so calm and untroubled.

All afternoon she had thought about Ross.

And she had decided that she couldn't go out with him again.

Ross thought he owned her. He really did.

And, she decided, he had no right to think that way.

She knew that Ross wouldn't give up, wouldn't stop pestering her.

But she had decided not to accept his apology. Not to forgive him again. Not to go out with him anymore.

Now, all she had to do was tell him.

Her heart racing, she cleared her throat and raised the phone to her face. "How are you feeling?" she asked.

"Better," he replied. "I'm still a little sore. That Denny is an animal."

"Yeah. I know," she said without warmth.

"What are you doing?" he asked.

"Talking to you," she replied.

"Listen, this afternoon — " he started.

"This afternoon, I meant what I said," Ashley told him, interrupting and talking rapidly.

"Huh? What's that supposed to mean?" His tone grew angry.

"It means I won't accept any apology from you."

"And what's that supposed to mean?"

"It means I'm not going out with you again."

"But, Ashley — "

"Good-bye, Ross. Have a good summer, okay?"

She hated the way she sounded, so cold, so heartless and uncaring.

But he had asked for it. He had promised at the beginning of the summer that he wouldn't be a jealous idiot.

"You didn't keep your promise, Ross," she said, her voice breaking.

She stifled a sob that wanted to burst from her chest.

She *did* care about him, after all.

"Hey, I promise it won't happen again. I just lost my temper. You know. I won't — "

"Bye, Ross."

She forced herself to click off the phone.

Then she dropped the phone to her lap and sat staring at it for a long moment, waiting for her heart to stop racing, waiting for her breathing to return to normal.

Finally, she picked up the phone and was about to set it down on her bed table when it rang. Startled, she nearly dropped it.

This is Ross again, she thought angrily.

He's so stubborn.

Why can't he believe that I mean it this time, that I really mean it?

"Hello?"

The voice in her ear wasn't Ross's.

It was husky, dry, a throaty whisper.

"Is this Ashley?"

"Yes?" Who can this be? Who do I know with this strange hoarse voice?

"Stay away from Brad."

"Huh?" Ashley cried. "I can't hear you very well. Can you speak up a little? Who *is* this?"

"Stay away from Brad," the husky voice repeated in its raspy whisper. *"Or you will die."*

"Huh? This is a joke, right?"

Ashley wanted to believe it was a joke, but the voice was so serious, so strange, so grating in her ear.

A chill of fear streaked down her back. She realized she was gripping the phone so tight, her hand hurt.

"Ross — you're not funny," she said angrily. "This is really childish."

"It isn't childish. It is true," the voice rasped. *"I am already dead. You will be dead, too."*

Ashley suddenly believed she recognized the voice. "Sharon? Sharon — is it you?"

Silence.

"Sharon — why are you doing this? I thought you were Brad's cousin. I thought — "

*"I am not Sharon. I am dead. And I am warning
you. Only one warning. Stay away from Brad. Or
you will be dead — like me."*

The line went silent.

Ashley clicked off the phone and dropped it onto
he bed table.

She realized she was trembling all over.

That voice, she thought. That ghastly voice.

So empty. So completely empty and dry.

It really sounded *dead.*

19
A Secret

Ashley leaned on Brad's shoulder as they stepped out of the movie theater, their eyes adjusting to the brightness of the street lights. "I thought it was funny," she insisted.

"I know," Brad replied, rolling his eyes. "You were the only one laughing." He stopped to study the Coming Attractions posters on the theater wall.

"I didn't embarrass you, did I?" Ashley asked. "I can't help it. Chevy Chase just makes me laugh."

"You sure thought it was hilarious when he fell off the ladder," Brad said, shaking his head. "It wasn't even him. It was a stuntman."

"So what?" she declared. "It was funny."

The old movie theater, a squat brick building that recently had been turned into a six-plex, stood at the edge of town. Beyond its brightly lit marquee, the street was dark. Nearly all the shops and restaurants had closed for the night. A few couples drifted slowly up and down Main Street, peering into shop windows, enjoying the cool night air, which carried the smell of the ocean.

"Want to walk for a bit?" Brad asked.

"Sure," she said, smiling.

They stepped out from under the marquee and crossed the street. It was their third date, Ashley realized, and she was beginning to feel comfortable with Brad.

It hadn't been easy at first. She had found him to be surprisingly shy. And it was nearly impossible to get him to laugh, or even smile much.

But, she discovered, he was very intelligent, and he had an intensity, a seriousness about things that she admired.

"What are you thinking about?" he asked.

"Chevy Chase," she replied, and burst out laughing.

"Are you going to be laughing like that all night?" he asked.

"Probably."

"Look at those dogs." He pointed.

Two mangy houndlike dogs were trotting along the sidewalk side by side, looking like two human window-shoppers out for a stroll.

"They think it's their town," Brad said dryly. "They think it's all been put here to amuse them."

Ashley laughed. The dogs stopped together to gaze into a shop window. Then they resumed their walk. She watched them jog around the corner by the local savings bank and disappear. As she stared at the corner, she realized that someone was standing there, hidden in the shadows against the bank building.

He was there, staring back at her, watching her in the safety of the darkness.

And then he slipped away into the shadows and was gone.

Ross, she realized.

I saw you, Ross.

How stupid. How childish.

Was he following her on her dates? Spying on her?

All week Ashley had had a feeling that someone was watching her. A prickly feeling on the back of her neck when she walked in town, when she was sunbathing on the beach, when she went to meet Brad.

But every time she had turned around, had tried to discover who it was, no one had been there. She had dismissed the feeling, chalking it up to creeping paranoia.

But she wasn't going crazy. There *had* been someone spying on her.

Ross.

The big baby.

She felt like shouting out to him, calling his name, embarrassing him.

But the street was empty now. Ross had slipped away.

Is he going to follow me around *forever*? she wondered, feeling her anger grow.

And then she wondered: Did Ross make that

frightening call to me, warning me to stay away from Brad? Or did he get someone to make the call for him?

If he's childish enough to follow me around on my dates, he's childish enough to have made that call, she reasoned.

What a dumb practical joke.

Did Ross really think it would work? That it would keep me from going out with Brad?

If anything, the call had made Ashley more eager to go out with Brad.

So stupid, she thought. Such a stupid prank.

But the call had been on her mind ever since. Again and again, she had heard the husky, dry voice. The voice of the dead. Threatening her. Warning her.

So stupid.

Several times she had started to tell Brad about it. But each time she decided not to.

It would only trouble him, she decided. Only make him feel bad. Make him angry.

The voice had never called again. Ashley had decided to forget the whole thing. But that was easier said than done.

Every time the phone rang, she remembered the call, heard the eerie voice, and became angry and frightened all over again.

But now I really can forget it, Ashley thought, squeezing Brad's hand as they crossed the dark street. Seeing Ross lurking there against the bank wall, spying on her from the shadows, she realized that he *had* to be the caller.

It was so pitiful. Such a pitiful, desperate attempt to try to get her not to go out with Brad.

Having solved the mystery of the call, she could dismiss it from her mind.

With these thoughts stirring in her head, she walked, holding hands with Brad. Before she realized it, they had walked to the beach, empty and silent, the color of pearl under a bright full moon.

"Are you okay?" Brad asked suddenly, his expression concerned. "You're so quiet tonight."

"No, I'm fine," she protested. "I — I thought I saw someone back in town."

"Someone? Who?" He turned to face her, to stare into her eyes as if searching for the answers to his questions.

"Ross," she told him. "I think he's been following me or something."

"That's kind of sad," Brad said sympathetically. "Don't you think?"

Ashley nodded. "Yeah. And stupid."

"Have you talked to him since . . . since . . .?"

"No," Ashley replied, turning her eyes to the water. "I haven't talked to him in days. I really don't want to."

Black waves rose up and crashed along the shore. It was such a clear night, Ashley realized. There were a million stars in the purple sky. She didn't want to think about Ross. She wanted to enjoy being with Brad, enjoy the shadowy beauty of the beach, the magical night sky, so bright, so vast.

Suddenly, Brad pulled her face to his and kissed her.

Pleased, she closed her eyes and kissed him back.

When she pulled her face away, he clung to her, pulled her face back up to his, and kissed her again.

He's never done this before, Ashley thought, kissing him with her eyes wide open this time.

He seems so . . . needy.

She had to give a hard tug to break away.

He looked disappointed. His dark eyes caught the light of the full moon and filled with sudden excitement. "I want to . . . show you something," Brad said breathlessly.

Ashley took another step back to see him more clearly. She had never seen him like this. What was on his mind?

"It's something kind of special," he continued. "A secret."

She stared back at him, trying to guess what he was talking about. "A secret? What is it, Brad?"

He was breathing hard, nearly panting. "No one else knows about it," he said mysteriously. "I've never really trusted anyone. I mean, I've never trusted anyone enough to show it to them, to share it with them. But — "

"You're driving me bananas!" Ashley declared. "What are you talking about?"

Caught up in his own excitement, he didn't seem to hear her, didn't seem to recognize her impatience. "Can I tell you something?" he asked, his eyes wide with eagerness, leaning toward her, bringing his face very close to hers, his hands shoved deep into the pockets of his faded denims.

"Yeah, sure," she replied, feeling uncomfortable.

Brad hesitated, then plunged in with what he had to say. "I've never had a girlfriend before. I mean, really. I'm sixteen and I've never had a girlfriend. I mean, you're the first girl I could really *relate* to. Other girls didn't understand. But you're different, Ashley. You really are."

Whoa! Ashley thought. This is getting too intense.

What is he going to do — propose?

Why is he telling me all this? And why is he breathing so hard?

What is he leading up to?

She casually let her eyes roam the beach. No one. No one in sight. "What do you want to show me?" she asked, her growing fear edging into her voice.

"Something very exciting I discovered," Brad answered. "In the beach house." He gestured toward the dark structure at the end of the beach.

"The beach house?" Ashley nearly gasped at the sound of the words. "You want to take me to the beach house?"

"Yeah," he said, grabbing both of her hands and starting to pull her, an eager, imploring smile on his face.

Ashley held back. "What's in the beach house?"

"Come on," he insisted. "I'll show you. It's my

secret. You won't be sorry. Really."

Sorry.

A wave of fear swept over her.

Won't be sorry.

She thought of Kip and Lucy in the beach house.

She thought of finding Lucy's green scarf on the closet floor.

She thought of Kip's stories about the beach house. Stories about murders that supposedly took place there more than thirty years ago.

"Come on," Brad insisted, tugging her hand. "Come *on*."

Reluctantly, she followed him, feeling her throat tighten with dread, feeling her legs grow heavy, and her heart start to pound.

And now they were standing just below the deck, staring up at the old house. The beach house, so dark, so empty, so cold.

Why did he want to bring her here?

What was Brad's secret?

PART FIVE

Summer of 1956

20
Real Gone

"I just feel so bad," Buddy said as they trudged over the sand toward the beach house. "You know, about Maria and Stuart. It's just so awful. Two people I knew." His voice cracked with emotion.

Amy put a sympathetic hand on his shoulder, and they walked on in silence. The evening sky darkened to the color of charcoal. A few drops of cold rain hit Amy's head.

It's really going to storm, Amy thought. I probably shouldn't have come with Buddy. But the poor guy just looked so forlorn.

She thought of Ronnie and the twenty people that were coming to his summer house for a barbecue. They're all going to end up indoors, Amy thought, as she felt more raindrops.

The beach house loomed in front of them. Oh, well, Amy thought. At least Buddy and I can go inside and keep dry. She wondered if there was a phone inside where she could call her parents and tell them where she was.

"Do you think about them all the time?" Buddy asked, his voice still choked with emotion.

"I think about Maria a lot," Amy admitted. "But, sometimes, you know what I do? I force myself to think about other things."

"You do?" Buddy seemed surprised.

"Yeah. I just shut Maria out of my mind. Otherwise, I think I'd go crazy from sadness," Amy said. "The summer is ruined. It's been the worst summer of my life," she continued. "But we have to go on, right? I mean, what choice do we have?"

"I guess," Buddy said thoughtfully, staring straight ahead as the beach house hovered over them.

"I keep thinking of that song Jane Froman sings on TV every week. 'When You Walk Through a Storm, Keep Your Head Up High.' I know it's corny — but it helps me. It really does."

"I don't watch much TV," Buddy said quietly.

A gust of wind splashed raindrops in their faces.

"Didn't you see Elvis Presley on TV last night?" Amy asked.

"Who?"

"Elvis Presley. He's a new rock-and-roll singer. He was on that show last night with the two band-leaders. You know — Tommy and Jimmy Dorsey. And when Elvis Presley came out, all the girls in the audience started to scream and carry on. Didn't you see it?"

"No," Buddy said glumly. "Elvis Presley? That's kind of a stupid name, isn't it? Is he any good?"

"He's *gone!*" Amy gushed. "He's really *gone!*"

Buddy chuckled, his dark eyes filled with amusement.

At least I'm cheering him up a little, Amy thought. She shivered. The rain started to come down steadily, pattering noisily against the sand.

"Buddy, can we go inside? We're going to get drenched." She pointed up to the house.

He shrugged. "I kind of like it. It's refreshing, don't you think?"

"I'd really like to go inside," Amy insisted. "I had the sniffles this morning. I really don't want to catch cold."

"Well . . ." He seemed very reluctant.

"If you're worried about your parents or something . . ." Amy said, glancing up at the house, which appeared dark and empty.

"My mom isn't here," Buddy said quickly. "She had to . . . go somewhere." He changed his mind. "Okay. Let's go in. I don't want you to catch cold."

She followed him up to the deck, then around to the sliding-glass door, where they entered, closing the door behind them. It was warm inside, but it took Amy a little while to stop shivering.

"My hair is soaked. I must look like Little Orphan Annie," she said, pushing at her tight curls.

"No, you don't," Buddy replied, smiling. "You look like Marilyn Monroe."

Amy laughed. "Yeah, sure."

Her arms crossed over her chest, she began walking around the living room, checking out the furnishings. "I love everything in here," she said, gesturing to the vinyl and wrought-iron couch. "It's all so modern."

"Yeah, I guess," Buddy replied, his expression still one of amusement.

"And, gosh, look at the TV!" Amy gushed. "Such a big screen. Is it a sixteen-inch screen? Do you get good reception here? We can only get one channel at our cottage. And I have to keep moving the rabbit ears to get it to come in good."

"I don't really know," Buddy said, his smile fading. He walked to the sliding-glass door and stared out at the rain.

He's getting restless, Amy thought. Maybe I'm chattering too much. Maybe I'm boring him. He wishes he hadn't brought me here.

Well, I'm just trying to cheer him up.

What am I supposed to do?

"Okay if I look around the rest of the house?" she asked, heading toward the hall. "I just love exploring other people's houses."

He didn't reply, so she took herself on a short tour. To her surprise, the rest of the house was barely furnished. In fact, it didn't appear as if anyone had lived here at all.

"Hey, Buddy, this closet is enormous!" she called from the bedroom closet. "I can't even see the back of it! Buddy!"

A hand grabbed her shoulder roughly.

"Buddy?"

With startling force, he jerked her out of the closet.

"Hey —" she cried in surprise.

"Better stay out of there," he warned sternly, staring intensely into her eyes.

"Oh. Okay," Amy said, rubbing her shoulder as she backed out of the room. "Sorry. I really do think this house is neat."

"Yeah. Neat," he muttered, following right behind her as she made her way back to the living room.

She peered out through the glass door. The sky was as black as night, but the rain had slowed to a drizzle. Beneath the house, the crashing waves sent up a steady roar.

"It's like being on a boat," Amy said, turning and leaning her back against the door. "The house is just so neat."

"Yeah, you're neat, too," Buddy said, his expression turning sour.

Amy forced a giggle. "Now you're making fun of me, Buddy. Why are you making fun of me?"

"No, I mean it," he said, moving toward her, his hands on his hips, his eyes narrowed, locked on hers. "You're neat, Amy. You're gone. You're really *gone*."

A cold chill ran down Amy's back.

Something was wrong.

Something was wrong with Buddy. With the look on his face. With the way he was talking to her.

She didn't like this. He was scaring her now. He was deliberately *trying* to scare her.

"I'm going home now, Buddy," she said, staring back at him. "My parents will be worried. They expect me for dinner."

"But you're gone," Buddy said. "You're real gone, Amy."

"Buddy, please —" Still facing him, her hand grabbed for the door handle.

"Ronnie's gone," Buddy said, taking another step closer, still squinting at her, his face set, expressionless, cold as metal. "Ronnie's gone — and now you're gone."

"Ronnie's gone?" she stammered. "What do you mean?"

"Ronnie's gone," Buddy repeated. "He didn't make it home for his barbecue. He's gone. And now it's your turn."

As Buddy moved closer, Amy gasped and struggled to open the door. It wouldn't budge.

Without thinking, she pushed away from it, darted past Buddy, and into the kitchen.

"All gone," Buddy said, his eyes glassy now, like a store mannequin's, his expression just as wooden. "All gone, Amy."

I'm cornered here, Amy realized in her panic. I can't get away.

21
Amy Tricks Buddy

"Buddy — what's the matter? What are you going to do?" Amy cried, backing against the kitchen counter. Her eyes searched desperately for something she could use as a weapon — *anything* — but the kitchen was completely bare.

He stood in the entranceway to the kitchen, blocking any path of escape. His eyes were narrowed, studying her, enjoying her panic.

"You hurt my feelings," he said softly.

"Huh?" She groped for words, but her mind was suddenly blank, as if her fear had erased everything.

Think, think, think, she told herself.

Think of a way out of this. Think of a way to calm him down.

Calm him down?

He seemed perfectly calm, Amy realized to her horror.

She was the one about to shriek at the top of her

159

lungs. Buddy stood staring at her calmly from the doorway, speaking so quietly, she had to strain to hear.

"You shouldn't have made fun of me," he said. He raised a hand, examined a finger, and began picking at a hangnail, concentrating intently on the operation.

"But, Buddy, we were just joking," Amy blurted out in a voice she didn't recognize. "No one meant any harm."

"*You humiliated me!*" he screamed, losing his temper. Forgetting the hangnail, he balled both hands into fists. "Everyone made fun of me. Everyone. Why, Amy? Why'd you do it?"

Amy didn't reply. She gaped at him, open-mouthed.

"Maria made fun of me, too," Buddy said. "And she lied to me. So now she's gone."

"Did you . . . did you kill Maria?" Amy finally managed to stammer, feeling cold all over, cold and trembly.

"Of course," Buddy said, frowning.

"And Stuart?"

He nodded. "And Ronnie. Why did you do it, Amy? Why did you have to make fun of me?"

"Oh, no," Amy moaned, and grabbed the countertop to keep from sinking to her knees.

She felt so weak, too weak to stand. Too weak to face Buddy.

"I'm waiting for an answer," he said sharply.

"Buddy —" She was panting so hard, it was

nearly impossible to choke out any words. "Buddy, people play jokes on people. It isn't serious. It doesn't mean anything."

He stared at her coldly and didn't reply.

"Why did you kill them, Buddy? Because of some stupid practical jokes? Because of a little fun? Why did you kill them?"

"Because it's so easy," Buddy said, a strange, lopsided smile forming on his face. "So easy."

"That's why?"

"And because it really doesn't matter," he added with a sneer.

"Huh? Doesn't matter?"

He's crazy, she realized.

He's a crazy murderer.

It doesn't matter what I say. I won't be able to reason with him.

He killed all my friends. Killed them because of some jokes.

And now he's going to kill me.

Again, her eyes darted around the kitchen in search of something to use against him. But there wasn't even a potholder. Not a spoon. The counter was bare, as were the shelves by the window.

The window.

Could she pull it open and yell for help?

Probably.

She could yell for help until she was blue in the face.

But no one could hear her over the rush of the ocean, the roar of the wind.

No one was within miles, anyway.

Calling for help was out.

I've got to keep him talking, she thought. Got to keep him talking till I think of a way to escape.

"What do you mean it doesn't matter?" she asked, locking her eyes on his, trying to determine if he really was going to come after her. "How can you kill people — people you know — and say it doesn't matter?"

"It doesn't matter," Buddy said slowly, as if talking to a three-year-old, "because I don't live here anyway."

"Huh? You mean you don't live in this beach house?"

He shook his head and snickered quietly. It seemed to strike him as funny. "No one lives in this beach house," he said mysteriously.

How am I going to get out? Amy asked herself, trying to think clearly, trying to clear the fog of panic so that she could make a plan.

Think, think, *think*.

Buddy took a step into the kitchen, his fists balled tightly at his sides.

"If you don't live here, where do you live?" Amy asked.

Keep stalling. Keep him talking.

It's your only chance.

Oh, Amy, you were so stupid, she scolded herself. You were right at the door. You were so close to escape.

Why did you run to the kitchen?

Why did you run to a room where there's no way out?

"Where do you really live?" she repeated, her voice high-pitched, revealing her terror.

He didn't reply.

Keep talking, Buddy, she pleaded silently. *Please* keep talking.

"No, really," she insisted. "Tell me. If you don't live here, where do you live?"

"No one lives here," Buddy said in a flat, frightening tone. "Everyone dies here."

He took another step toward her.

He was halfway into the room.

I have to try to trick him, Amy thought. I don't have much time.

She could only think of the oldest trick in the book.

Suddenly, she raised her eyes above Buddy's shoulder, gazed into the other room, and cried out in surprise.

"Ronnie! You're still alive! You're okay!"

Stunned, Buddy spun around to look.

And in that moment, Amy pushed herself away from the counter and made a run for the door.

22

Race for Freedom

Amy shoved Buddy hard as she ran past him.

He cried out, more in surprise than in pain.

She stumbled by him, arms outstretched toward the door.

He hesitated for only a second, then moved after her.

Reaching the glass door, she pulled the handle with both hands.

She was breathing so hard, her chest ached.

She could feel the blood pulsing in her temples.

The door resisted. She tugged again, harder, and it slid open.

And she was out on the deck, slippery from the rain.

I'm out of there! I'm *out!* she told herself happily.

But there was no time to celebrate. He was right behind her. She heard his sneakers clump across the wooden deck as she leapt down the stairs and onto the sand. And kept running.

Where was he?

Right behind? Gaining on her?

Her chest about to explode with pain, her legs so heavy, so heavy, she had to force them to take every step. She glanced back.

Saw him pick up the long-handled shovel from against the side of the house.

Saw him carry it in one hand as he came running after her, his eyes wild with fury, his mouth open in a silent scream.

"Help me! Somebody — please help me!"

Her words, shouted at the top of her lungs, seemed to fly right back to her, blown back by the wind.

She ran over the wet sand, her sandals kicking up clumps as they moved.

He was getting closer.

Keep going, keep going!

"Help! Please — somebody!"

But the beach was deserted. No one. Not even a sea gull to watch their desperate race. To hear her cries.

Over the sand, cold, wet sand crunching under her sandals. The ocean crashed to her right. The empty dunes rolled to her left.

No one. No one around.

The rain started again.

And he was gaining. She could hear his breathing, loud, rhythmic groans. She could hear his sneakers thudding over the sand.

Her chest was about to burst.

She knew it would burst. It hurt so much.

Everything hurt.

Keep going, keep going!

There's got to be someone. Someone walking on the beach.

Someone who can stop him.

Someone who can save her from him.

His groans grew louder, closer.

She was panting now, too. Panting and crying.

And the wind tossed the cold rain into her face.

She leaned into it, squinting against the rain.

He was so close behind now.

Closer. Closer.

She cried out, a wordless shriek, as she fell. Stumbled forward and landed hard on her elbows and knees.

She looked up to see him raise the shovel with both hands.

With a fierce groan, he swung the heavy metal blade at her head.

23

It Really Doesn't Matter

When Amy opened her eyes from the darkness, blacker and deeper than any darkness she had ever seen, the pain lingered.

The back of her head throbbed. The vibrating, ringing pain ran down the back of her neck, all the way down her back. So much pain, she closed her eyes again.

The feel of the water brought her back.

The cold shock of it.

Her eyes went wide when she realized she was waist deep in the ocean.

The green water leapt at her, pushed her, crept up on her, then pulled back only to leap again.

It was only when she tried to swim that she realized her hands were tied. She twisted around to discover they were tied with a heavy rope, tied to a wooden post of some sort.

She tried to cry out, but the water leapt again, and she swallowed a mouthful. Choking and cough-

ing, she struggled to catch her breath, spitting away
the briny taste.

The pain lingered, her head ringing like the inside
of a bell. But she was wide awake now. Awake and
alert.

And she knew where she was.

She knew she was under the beach house, her
hands tied tightly behind her, tied to one of the
stilts.

And she knew the tide was coming in. The waves
were leaping higher. The water was up over her
waist.

She saw it all so clearly now. But the pain
wouldn't allow her to think. The ringing pain
wouldn't allow her to try to make a plan.

She started to scream, an animal howl, high-
pitched and frightened, that barely carried over the
steady rush of the water.

Tossing her head back out of the thrashing
waves, she howled like a frightened animal. Like
an animal caught in a trap.

She stopped howling when she saw Buddy standing in the water, the water halfway up the legs of
his jeans. Buddy, hands on his knees, by the side
of the house, peering in at her.

Watching her fear.

Watching her pain.

Smiling.

She stopped screaming and stared back at him,
struggling to loosen the ropes that held her in place.

"No one can hear you," Buddy said calmly, casually, as if commenting on the weather.

"Let me go!" Amy pleaded.

The pain at the back of her head made her wince and cry out. What was the warm trickle down the back of her neck? Was it blood?

"No one can save you now," Buddy said matter-of-factly. He took a step closer, the water creeping up to the knees of his jeans.

"Let me *go*! Please, Buddy!"

"You left me in the ocean," Buddy said, ignoring her shrill, terrified cry. "All of you. You left me in the ocean. You took my swim trunks and left me there."

"But, Buddy —"

"And then you walked away. You just walked away."

Shaking his head, he turned and started toward the sand.

"No — Buddy! Come back! Come back!" Amy begged.

He kept walking, his back to her now, his back to the rising, leaping waves.

"Buddy — stop! Where are you going?"

He stopped and turned back to her. "I'm walking away, Amy. I'm walking away, just like you did."

"No — Buddy! You can't! You can't leave me here! Buddy — please! You *can't*!"

He leaned under the house, one hand on the wooden stilt.

He's coming back, she thought.

He's going to save me now.

He isn't going to let me drown. He only wanted to frighten me.

"Don't worry, Amy," he said quietly, so quietly, she had to strain to hear him over the rushing water.

Don't worry, she thought. He's going to save me now.

He's going to untie me.

He isn't going to leave me here.

"Don't worry," he repeated. "The tide's coming in really fast. It'll be over your head in a few minutes. You won't suffer long."

He turned away again.

She could see only his legs. The wet denim jeans clinging to his legs. The white sneakers splashing to shore.

And then she couldn't see him at all.

And the water had risen to her shoulders.

"See you later, alligator," she heard him call from somewhere behind her. "You're a real gone chick. But now I've got to go home."

Buddy climbed the deck steps quickly and let himself into the house. He slid the glass door shut, closing out the sound of Amy's last terrified screams.

PART SIX

This Summer

24
Brad Gets Serious

Ashley stopped at the deck steps and looked up at the old beach house, a black shadow against the violet sky.

I don't want to go in there with Brad, she decided, feeling a shiver of fear descend her back.

Oil-dark waves washed under the house, lapping against the wooden stilts. The wind off the ocean was strong and heavy with the smell of fish.

"Come on. I'm dying to show you this," Brad insisted, tugging her hand, trying to pull her up the stairs.

The house shifted suddenly, creaking loudly, as if warning her to stay away.

"Brad, it's so late —" she started, trying to pull away.

"Come on, Ashley. I *have* to show this to you."

"My parents will be really pushed out of shape," she said. "I've got to get home."

His face fell into a disappointed pout.

"Tell me what's inside," she said quickly. "*Tell* me the secret. You can show it to me some other time."

His unhappy expression didn't change. He turned his eyes to the dark, tossing waves.

"No. I have to show you," he said in a low voice. He sat down on the top step, the old wood creaking under his weight. He patted the spot beside him, motioning for her to join him.

"Brad, it's getting cold," Ashley protested.

But she couldn't bear the unhappy pout on his face. Obediently, she sat down beside him on the step.

"I really want to share this secret with you," Brad said, staring at the ocean. "I would never share it with anyone else."

Ashley shifted uncomfortably on the hard step. From somewhere, the pungent smell of gasoline invaded her nostrils.

"Brad, you shouldn't get too serious," she warned.

He turned to her, his eyes revealing confusion.

"About me, I mean," Ashley said, tugging awkwardly at a strand of her blonde hair. "You shouldn't get too serious. I mean, we've only gone out a few times."

"Hey, I *am* serious," he replied. "I'm very serious, Ashley." He slid his arm around her waist. "I'm always serious," he said. "Haven't you noticed that about me?"

"Why do I smell gasoline?" Ashley asked in a

not very subtle attempt to change the subject.

Brad shrugged. "Maybe there were some powerboats in the water around here. Some jet skis or something."

"Brad, could we —?" Cold and uncomfortable, troubled by Brad's insistence on taking her into the beach house, Ashley really wanted to start for home.

"I want to tell you something about me," Brad said, his arm still protectively around her waist. "Maybe it'll help you understand me a little."

"Well . . ." She realized he was ignoring her discomfort.

His mind seemed to be somewhere else, lost in his own thoughts. His eyes narrowed, focused on the distance, as if he were seeing something there, something that only he could see.

"The men in my family have always been explorers," he began, still staring straight ahead. "In one way or another, that is. My great-grandfather really *was* an explorer. He sailed to Africa when he was in his late forties. He went up the Amazon, photographing different tribes. Some of his photos are in a museum in Washington, D.C."

"Wow," Ashley said appreciatively. "How do you know all this?"

"My father told my brother and me about it," Brad said. He raked a hand back through his dark hair, then continued. "My grandfather was an explorer, too. A different kind of explorer. He owned a textile mill. He did his exploring right in the mill.

He explored new kinds of fabrics. Artificial fabrics."

"You mean like rayon and nylon?" Ashley asked. She had once done a home ec report on polyesters and other artificial materials.

"Yeah," Brad nodded. "That's how my granddad made his fortune. He became the rayon king of the world." He chuckled. "You see our big, fancy summer house, our tennis court, and swimming pool? The Jaguars and Mercedes in the drive? That's all because of my granddad. That's all because of rayon."

Why is he telling me all this? Ashley wondered, shifting her weight again on the uncomfortable step.

Something dark fluttered near. She saw a shadow dart low over the beach. A bat?

"Did you see that?" she asked, her voice a whisper.

"I guess you could call my father an explorer, too," Brad continued, so caught up in remembering his story that he didn't hear her.

Or didn't choose to hear her.

"A few years after my brother Johnny was born, my dad left us. Just didn't come home one day. I guess you could say he was exploring other lifestyles or something." He snickered. Bitter laughter. "We saw him from time to time. And he made sure we had more money than any twenty families would ever need. But he was too busy *exploring* to spend any time with us."

"That's terrible," Ashley said sympathetically.

"Yeah," Brad agreed, with even more bitterness.

"I haven't met Johnny," Ashley said, still wondering where this story was leading, why Brad was telling it to her.

Was it part of the secret he wanted to share?

"You won't meet Johnny," Brad said flatly, all expression fading from his face. He closed his eyes for a brief moment, then stared intently at Ashley.

"I think Johnny may have been the biggest explorer of all of us," he told her. "He was always desperate to explore everything he saw. *Everything*. I always had trouble keeping up with Johnny. I was the older brother. Two years older. But I couldn't keep up with him. I really couldn't.

"I was older, but I was the one who always tagged along, always followed Johnny."

He stopped for a moment. Ashley realized he was breathing heavily, excitedly.

She started to say something. But he continued his story.

"Johnny was always the most fun-loving kid. I was always the serious one. He was a real joker. He just loved to goof on people. But the main thing that was special about Johnny was his curiosity."

"He had a scientific mind?" Ashley asked.

"No. He just had this incredible curiosity. Like a true explorer. I mean, show Johnny a door, and he *had* to know what was behind it. Show him an *open* door, and he'd be through it in a flash.

"He was curious about everything," Brad continued, his voice breaking. He cleared his throat and continued. "Johnny was always taking things apart just to see how they worked. Things like radios and TVs, and our piano. He drove my mother bananas. He really did. But he just had to know what was behind things.

"I tried to be like him," Brad said with growing sadness. "I tried. But I just wasn't Johnny. I worshipped the kid. I admit it. And then when he died —"

He stopped abruptly.

Ashley didn't know what to say. Was he waiting for her to react?

She had already guessed that Johnny was dead from the way Brad was talking about him in the past tense.

"How did he die?" she asked finally.

"It wasn't my fault," Brad replied, the light fading in his eyes. "It wasn't my fault, but I blamed myself. For a long, long time. I still blame myself, I guess." He sighed, then continued, speaking more slowly, more carefully. "I was supposed to watch him. But I just couldn't keep up with him. No one could. They were building a new house, an enormous new house in the cul-de-sac down from our house. Johnny couldn't resist new houses. He loved to explore them, to climb around in them while they were empty, while they were still going up.

"By the time I realized he had gone into the new house, by the time I got there and went inside, he was dead." Brad's eyes burned into Ashley's. He stared at her as if trying to make sure she believed him, trying to make sure she accepted his story.

"I didn't even hear him scream. He must have screamed. He fell from the second floor to the basement. The floor wasn't finished. He fell straight down and broke his neck on the concrete basement floor."

Brad was breathing hard now, his chest heaving. He turned his face away.

They sat in silence for a long while.

"I've tried to be like Johnny," Brad said finally, very softly, still avoiding Ashley's eyes. "I tried to be an explorer like Johnny. But I'm not Johnny. I know it. I can't be Johnny. I'm too serious. I don't have his mind, his energy, his *anything*. And ever since Johnny died, I just take everything too hard. Everything."

"You can't blame yourself," Ashley said, cringing from the hollowness of her words, but not knowing what else to say. "It was an accident, that's all. A terrible accident."

"Then at the start of the summer, *I* decided to go exploring," Brad said, not seeming to hear her. "I saw this old beach house here at the edge of the beach. Empty all these years. It must have been built nearly forty years ago. People told me that no one has ever lived in it."

"That's the same story I heard," Ashley said, turning to look up at the dark windows on the side of the house, staring back at her like bug eyes.

"So I decided to do some exploring," Brad said. "Just like Johnny would have done. Early one morning, I came here. There was no one on the beach.

Just a few early morning joggers. It was early June. Still cold in the morning. Anyway, I came up here. I went inside the house. And I did some exploring."

He stood up suddenly, grabbed her hands, and pulled her to her feet.

"Come on. I have to show you what I found."

His eyes glowed at her excitely. An eager smile spread across his face.

"I found something incredible in there," he said.

Still Ashley resisted.

I really don't want to go in there, she thought, thinking of Kip and Lucy.

Thinking of how dark and frightening the old house looked.

I really don't want to go in.

But then she saw something stir back in the low dunes.

Someone was in the tall grass, crouched there.

She saw just a shadow, a quick movement. And she knew someone was there.

Ross, she knew.

Ross. Still spying on me. That childish idiot.

She could feel her anger grow inside her chest.

Okay, Ross. You want to spy on me? she thought. I'll give you something to spy on.

She took Brad's arm. "Okay," she whispered. "Let's go inside. Show me this amazing secret."

Brad smiled and led the way. "You won't believe it," he said excitely.

He slid open the glass door, and Ashley followed him into the darkness.

25
Brad's Secret

Ashley stopped in front of the door. "It's too dark, Brad. I can't see a thing."

She felt his hand on her shoulder. "Wait here. Don't move. I'll be right back."

She heard his footsteps cross the creaking floor as he disappeared into the darkness. A few seconds later, she saw a wavering cone of yellow light darting across the ceiling and over the wall, like Tinkerbell in *Peter Pan*.

"I hid this flashlight under the kitchen sink," Brad said, smiling as he returned to view. "It's pretty bright, huh? It's a halogen light."

He motioned for her to join him in the living room. "Look around," he said, speaking loudly to be heard over the rush of water beneath the house. "It's really awesome."

"All this old fifties-style furniture is pretty amazing," Ashley said, obediently glancing around the big front room, her eyes following the bright light of Brad's flashlight. "Even an old TV. Look how small the screens were back then."

"Sixteen inches," Brad said, training the beam of light on the old TV.

"But I've been in here before, remember?" Ashley reminded him.

"Yeah, I know," Brad replied, smiling.

"So what's the secret?" she asked impatiently.

I don't like it in this house, she thought, moving her eyes along the shadowy furniture. I don't like the way the house sways, the way you can hear the ocean under the floor. It's like you're on an old boat, traveling *nowhere*.

"I'll show you the secret," Brad said, startling her by stepping up right beside her. "But first I want to tell you how much I like you."

"Thanks," Ashley said, flustered. Then she quickly added, "I like you, too."

And before she could back away, Brad had his arms around her and was pressing his mouth against hers.

The flashlight clattered to the floor and rolled away.

Ashley gave in to his kiss. Then she began to kiss him back.

But after a while, his intensity began to frighten her.

She tried to pull her face away, tried to take a step back. But he pulled her closer, held her more tightly with surprising strength, and continued to kiss her.

Harder, harder.

Until it was no longer a kiss.

Until it felt hostile, angry, like an assault.

Ashley raised both hands to his chest, and pushed.

Still he wouldn't back away.

She pushed harder and arched her neck, turning her face away from him. "Brad — please — "

Breathing hard, his breath hot against her cheek, it took him a while to recover. "I care about you, Ashley," he said finally.

She stepped back, relieved that he had let go of her.

"The surprise," she reminded him. "Was *that* the surprise?"

He bent to pick up the flashlight. When he stood up, she saw the hurt expression on his face. "Don't you trust me?"

She forced a laugh, trying to lighten things up. "Brad — how long are you going to keep me in suspense? Please, bring out the surprise."

His expression remained set, almost grim. "I can't bring it out. You'll have to come see it."

"Okay," she said, unable to hide her impatience. "Lead the way. It's really getting late, you know. Where is it?"

He was holding the light at his waist, shining it up at his face. In the yellow light, he looked eerie, frightening, like a Halloween vampire. His eyes seemed to glow with unnatural excitement.

"It's in the bedroom," he told her. "Come with me."

"Whoa!" Ashley held back. "The bedroom?"

After that uncomfortably intense kiss, Ashley was reluctant to follow Brad into the bedroom. "No. I don't think so, Brad."

"Ashley — come *on*!" he cried, whining, his voice rising several octaves. "You *have* to see this! I've never shown it to anyone else."

"Let's come back tomorrow," she suggested, feeling more than a little frightened. "You know. In daylight."

"Ashley." He said her name disapprovingly, shaking his head, his eyes still aglow in the cone of light from the flashlight. "I'm not going to try anything. Really."

She hesitated, studying his face.

"Don't hurt my feelings," he said softly. "I've told you more about me tonight than I've ever told anyone. Please. I trusted you. Now you have to trust me."

"Okay," she said, too weary to resist any longer. "Okay. I'm coming."

She took a deep breath and followed him into the hallway, the circle of light darting across the wood floor as they walked.

He turned quickly into the first bedroom, tilting the light to the ceiling so that it reflected over the entire room.

"I've been here before," Ashley said, examining the room in the dim light. Nothing had changed since the last time she had been there.

The day she had discovered Lucy's scarf.

"This way," Brad said, pointing the light to the closet.

"Huh?"

Moving quickly, he slid open the closet door. He stepped inside. The light dimmed as he entered. It seemed to lose some of its brightness, the yellow light turning to gray.

"Come on. Get in," he called.

"Get in the closet?" Ashley took a few steps toward him, then hesitated.

"Yeah. Get in," he called impatiently. "Hurry."

She stood just beyond the closet door. The enormous closet. So dark, even with the flickering, diving light of the flashlight. So deep. So endless.

"Brad — come *on*. Why do I have to get in the closet?" she demanded.

"Just *do it*!" he snapped.

She peered in. The gray light seemed to fade before it reached the closet walls.

"*Do it! Get in!*"

"No," she told him. "I don't want to."

"Come in here — now!" he commanded in a sharp, angry shout.

He grabbed her hand roughly and pulled her inside.

26
Who's in the Closet?

Ashley found herself encircled by the eerie gray light, as if she had stepped into a cloud.

Once she was in the closet, Brad let go of her hand. He turned his back to her and took a few steps, appearing to fade into a gray mist.

"Brad — stop!" Ashley called, frightened, her voice strangled, muffled.

It was cold inside the closet, and damp. The air felt heavy as she breathed, and she found herself gulping mouthfuls of it.

"Follow me," Brad instructed from the shadows, his voice still sharp. It was a command, not a request.

"Brad, I don't want to," Ashley insisted, hanging back. "I don't like this."

"Don't like what?"

Even though he was only a few feet in front of her, she had to squint to see him among the shifting gray shadows.

"I can't see," she protested. "I can't see where I'm going. I can't see anything. Not even the closet walls."

"I told you this was incredible," Brad insisted. "Get away from the door. You *have* to follow me."

"Just wait a second, okay?" Ashley pleaded. "Why can't you explain to me what we're doing in here? Why do you have to be so mysterious? You're *frightening* me. Really!"

Suddenly he loomed in front of her, bursting from the gray. His features were drawn in a tight frown, his dark eyes flashing angrily.

He grabbed her shoulder. Hard. And tightened his fingers around her until the shoulder throbbed with pain.

"Stop acting like a frightened baby," he said, leaning close to her, spitting the words in her face.

"Let go," she cried, the pain forcing her to whimper.

He loosened his grip only a little.

"Let go of me, Brad. I mean it. I'm leaving now."

"No, you're not," he insisted, his expression cold, his words low and deliberate. "You've already come too far."

"Too far? What on earth are you *talking* about?" she shrieked.

"Follow me."

As he squeezed her shoulder, Ashley began to see colors, flashing oranges and yellows, faint at first, then growing brighter.

Brad let go of her shoulder, grabbed her hand

quickly, tightening his grip on her — and pulled her hard.

As he pulled, the flickering orange and yellow light grew closer, brighter.

What is going *on*? Ashley wondered.

Brad pulled her deeper into the closet.

Then, to her horror, Ashley felt a hand, another hand, a cold hand, a stranger's hand, grab her around the waist from behind.

27
A Surprise House Guest

Ashley screamed.

She sucked in a deep breath and screamed again.

The flickering orange and yellow light came from a kerosene torch. The flames dipped close, licked at her face.

"Whoa!" Brad cried out, startled, and dropped her hand.

The arm around her waist tightened and pulled her back.

Away from Brad.

Back. Back.

Ashley was too frightened to resist.

The flames danced just above her. The gray shadows seemed to pull away.

Back. Back. Following the flickering light.

And then she was out of the closet. Back in the bedroom.

The torch dipped and whispered, then floated back up.

Her chest heaving, her breath caught in her throat, Ashley turned to see who had pulled her from Brad, from the gray mist of the closet.

She stared into the bright flames.

The person holding the torch was hidden in the darkness behind it.

"Help! Oh, help me!" Ashley cried, too terrified to even realize that she was speaking aloud.

"Hey — " Brad's head poked out of the closet, his eyes wide with fury. "What's going on?" He emerged in the closet doorway, his fists balled tightly at his side, poised for a fight.

Ashley staggered backwards, away from the torch. She backed into the wall, braced herself against it, her hands to her face, and didn't move.

Brad squinted at the torch, the flickering orange and yellow light reflecting in his eyes, dancing across his angry face.

"You?" he cried, suddenly recognizing the person holding the torch. "What are you doing here?" His voice suddenly revealed more amazement than anger.

Ashley's eyes began to adjust to the new light.

A white uniform came into view. Then the torch illuminated dark hair, streaked with gray.

A woman's face. Staring unblinking at Brad.

"Mary — " Brad called to the family servant. "Mary — answer me! What are you doing here?"

The housekeeper didn't reply.

She didn't move. She didn't blink.

Then slowly, she lowered the torch, pointing it toward him.

He started to take a step out of the closet.

"Get back," she said, her voice tight but controlled.

"Mary, I'm afraid you don't belong here," Brad said, staring at her warily. Again, he took a tentative step toward her.

She moved quickly, lowering the torch, thrusting it forward, threatening him with it.

Brad cried out in surprise and ducked back.

"Don't come out, Buddy," she ordered Brad in the same even, controlled tone.

The torchlight caught the hatred in her eyes, dark, weary eyes.

"Don't come out, Buddy. You're never coming out again."

28
Scars

Ashley sank to her knees, staring at the angry confrontation between Brad and the servant.

"Stay back, Buddy. I'm warning you. I'll torch you without a second's hesitation," Mary said, gesturing with the fiery torch.

"Buddy? Why do you keep calling Brad *Buddy?*" Ashley managed to cry.

Mary kept her eyes on Brad. "Buddy is his nickname. Brad has always been called Buddy. Haven't you, *Buddy?*" She pronounced the name as if it were some kind of horrible curse.

Struggling to regain his composure, Brad propped his hands against the frame of the closet door and peered out at Mary. "No one has called me Buddy in years," he said, his voice trembling despite his struggle to appear calm. "How did you know that, Mary? Who *are* you, anyway?"

The question angered her. She cried out in disgust and swung the torch in front of her, leaving a smoky trail of color in the air.

"Who am I?" She glared at him.

Ashley noticed that she was wearing the same unusually styled uniform, with the heavy, long sleeves and the white blouse with the collar up to her chin.

"Who *am* I, Buddy?" She twisted her features in disgust.

I've got to get out of here, Ashley thought, turning her eyes to the doorway.

I don't know what's going on here.

But I can feel the hatred. It's as hot as the flame on Mary's torch.

She's crazy with anger.

Crazy.

She could even *kill* Brad or Buddy or whatever his name is.

I've got to get out of here, get help.

But Ashley didn't move. Her fear held her in place. Her curiosity held her there, crouched on her knees, against the bedroom wall.

Mary took a step toward the closet. Then another. She held the torch in front of her, drew it under her chin. Her face seemed to enlarge. It seemed to float, to hover in the smoky air, shadowy and orange.

"Don't you recognize me, Buddy?" Mary asked, her dark eyes surrounded by shifting shadows, glaring at Brad like snowman eyes, cold and dead.

"No!" he cried, his face revealing his fear. "Get back, Mary! Stay away from me!"

She took another step toward the closet, holding the torch at her waist.

"You really don't know who I am?"

"No!" Brad repeated. "I mean it, Mary. Stay away. Don't come any closer."

Ignoring his warning, she took another step. She was only a few feet from him now.

I've got to get out of here, Ashley thought.

I've got to get help.

She pulled herself to her feet. But she didn't move away from the wall.

She couldn't.

She had to see the scene played out.

Why was Brad so afraid of Mary? Why did Mary hate Brad so much?

"I'm warning you, Mary — " Brad cried, holding up both hands as if to shield himself from her.

She stared at him, ghostlike, her entire body appearing to flicker and bend with the torch flame.

"Take a good look at me, Buddy. Do you recognize me now?"

"No. No, I don't!" Brad screamed. "Get out! Get out of here!"

"Maybe this will help you remember me," she said, her eyes burning darkly into his.

With startling quickness, she reached her free hand up to the collar of her blouse. "Maybe this will help your memory."

The ripping sound made Ashley jump as Mary

tore open her blouse. Buttons clicked and rolled across the wooden floor.

Tearing violently at the sleeves, Mary pulled off the blouse and tossed it to the floor, revealing her bra.

And her scars.

Red and purple scars.

Some raised up, like welts. Some etched deeply into her skin.

The scars spread over her chest, across both shoulders, down her arms.

Ashley cried out and shut her eyes.

"Do you recognize me now?" Mary demanded of Brad.

Brad stared back at her, stared at the scars, at her disfigured body.

"Yes, it's me!" she declared triumphantly. "It's Maria! You killed me in 1956!"

29
Secret of the Beach House

The room grew silent, so silent that Ashley could hear the hiss of the torch, the lick of the flames.

She heard the slap of the waves against the stilts below. The hushed, steady roar of the sea wind.

We're sailing away, she thought, feeling the beach house sway. We're sailing away from this world, away from the real world.

"Brad, I don't understand!" Ashley called across the swaying room. "What is she *saying*?"

But Brad didn't seem to hear her. His eyes locked in disbelief on Maria. On her strangely victorious smile. On the scars that covered her body.

"You can't be," he uttered, his voice barely a whisper. "You can't be Maria. Maria was sixteen. You're old. You're — "

"I'm in my fifties, Buddy," Maria said, steadying the torch in front of her. "You're right. I'm old. Older tnan my years. Thanks to you."

"But — but — "

"I've had to wait a long time to pay you back," Maria said, her voice trembling with anger. "A long, long time. But . . . I've been patient. And, now, here I am."

"No!" he screamed. "You *can't* be!"

"What's the matter?" she asked, taunting him with mock sympathy. "You're not glad to see me, Buddy?"

"You're *dead*!" Buddy declared.

Ashley couldn't stand it any longer. "What is going on?" she screamed. She pushed herself away from the wall and made her way toward Maria. "Will somebody explain to me what you're talking about?"

Maria turned, a startled look on her face, as if seeing Ashley for the first time.

"Don't tell her anything!" Brad screamed, more a plea than an order.

"I'll tell her *everything*," Maria said, her triumphant smile returning.

"Tell me *what*?" Ashley demanded.

"Buddy learned the secret of this beach house," Maria said in a low, confidential voice.

"The secret?" Ashley glanced at Buddy, whose face reflected his horror and disbelief, then turned her eyes back to Maria.

"Buddy learned why no one has ever lived here, why no one ever will," Maria continued. "And now you will learn the house's secret, too."

She paused, as if gathering strength to reveal

the secret. Brad made a sudden move toward her, but she forced him back by thrusting the torch flame at his chest.

"I told you, Buddy. You're not coming out of there," she warned.

He scowled. "You're crazy! Don't listen to her, Ashley."

"Please — tell me about this house," Ashley pleaded.

"The house is a way station," Maria explained. "It was built on a time warp."

"Huh?" Ashley cried out. "A *what*?"

"A time warp," Maria repeated patiently. "The house is a way station between today . . . and 1956. Buddy, or Brad, as you call him, went exploring inside this house a few months ago, and he discovered the secret."

"You mean you can travel back to 1956 from this house?" Ashley asked, trying to believe Maria's words.

"No — it's not true! *It's not true!*" Brad cried.

But his desperation told Ashley that it *was* true.

Maria nodded solemnly. "Yes. Buddy discovered that he could go back to 1956. You step into the closet. You walk and walk through a heavy gray fog. It seems as if you're walking forever. But when you finally emerge from the fog, you are back in 1956."

"You can go back to 1956 and then return?" Ashley asked. "You can go and come back just by walking?"

Maria shook her head. "No. Going back in time is easy, just a long gray walk. But moving forward in time is hard. Somehow Buddy learned how to move forward, how to get back to his own time." Deep sadness crept into her voice. "It took me all of my life to figure out how to get here, how to follow Buddy to the future, to his time."

"Ashley, you don't believe any of this, do you?" Brad called from the closet doorway. "It's crazy — right? She's crazy."

"I believe it," Ashley replied, her eyes trained on Maria. "She's telling me the truth."

"Thank you," Maria said softly.

Ashley gasped as she had a sudden realization. "Oh, no," she uttered. "I know what happened to Kip and Lucy."

"Kip and Lucy? The two kids who disappeared?" Maria asked. "Were they in this beach house?"

"Yes," Ashley said, swallowing hard. "They must have discovered the closet, gotten curious about it. They must have stepped in, exploring, and walked back to 1956."

"And then they couldn't find their way back," Maria said, continuing Ashley's thought. "It's so hard to get back."

"It's tricky, okay," Brad said, snickering. "Kip and Lucy are probably in their fifties by now. Lord knows where they are!" He chuckled. He seemed to find the idea very amusing.

"How awful," Ashley muttered, shaking her

head. She turned back to Maria. "Why do you hate
Brad so much?"

"Ashley — I can't believe you're swallowing this
baloney!" Brad cried, sounding frantic. "Can't you
see she's wacko?"

"Buddy came back to 1956," Maria said, ignoring
his protests. "He made friends with me and with
three of my friends. Amy, Ronnie, and Stuart. We
had fun for a while. But then something went
wrong. Buddy got insulted. He went out of his mind
or something. Something must have snapped. He
went out of control. And then . . . he killed us. One
by one."

"No!" Ashley cried, raising her hands to her face
in horror.

"It's not true!" Brad insisted. "Not true!"

"He killed us. Coldly. Cruelly," Maria continued,
her dark eyes fading with sadness. "Then he returned to the future. He escaped, free and clear.
Until now."

Ashley opened her mouth to say something, but
was interrupted.

With a loud, angry cry, Brad leapt from the
closet. Moving with startling speed, he dived at
Maria, his arms reaching out to grab the torch.

30
Flames

Maria, determined to have her revenge, didn't flinch or shrink back.

As Buddy leapt, she thrust the torch forward.

The flame sizzled against his shoulder.

His eyes reacted first, growing wide with shock and pain. And then he cried out, falling heavily to the floor with a *thud*. Grabbing his shoulder, his shirt smoking, he crawled back to the safety of the closet.

"I told you, Buddy," Maria said, breathing heavily, the torch poised in both hands, "you're never coming out of there. Never."

Brad, on his knees in the closet doorway, groaned, rubbing his shoulder. "I just wanted to be like Johnny," he wailed. "That's all I wanted. I wanted to explore like Johnny. So I walked through the closet. That's just what Johnny would have done. I went back there. I met you and your friends.

201

I was exploring. I was really doing it, just like Johnny."

He swallowed hard, waiting for his breathing to return to normal. "But you wouldn't let me be like Johnny. You had to tease me, make fun of me, torture me. You wouldn't give me a chance. You had to humiliate me. So . . . so . . ."

He was gulping air, struggling not to burst into loud sobs. "If Johnny had been there . . ." he started. He lowered his head.

There was a long silence in the room. Then Maria turned to Ashley. "I tried to warn you away from him," she said. "I tried to scare you away."

"It was *you* who called me?" Ashley cried.

Maria nodded. "I saw you with him at his house, playing tennis. I saw the way he looked at you. The same way he looked at me more than thirty years ago. I wanted to warn you about him."

"You said you were dead," Ashley remembered, chilled by the thought.

"I *am* dead," Maria replied softly, lowering her eyes. "At least, my heart is dead. Somehow my body has survived." She gestured to her scars. "What is left of it."

"What happened to you?" Ashley asked, staring at the disfigured flesh, the red and purple scars. "Did Buddy do that?"

"He might as well have," Maria replied bitterly. "He cut my arm and left me for the sharks. The sharks came. They did a good job. It hurt so much. Pain beyond pain. And so much blood. Such horror.

I dream about it every night. Every night."

She stopped, took a deep breath, then continued. "As he swam away, I started to drown. I was choking, swallowing water. The sharks wouldn't quit. I finally gave up trying to fight them. I went under for the second or third time. Suddenly I felt hands pulling me up, strong hands. Two fishermen pulled me into their small boat. They saved my life. I wished they'd let me drown."

She stared into the yellow flame. The memories had become too painful to speak. Turning back to Ashley, she began again in a low voice just above a whisper.

"The fishermen got me to a doctor. They notified my aunt, my poor, horrified aunt. I was rushed to a hospital. I don't know how long I was there. Months and months. More than a year. When I got out, I was so ugly. So ugly, so deformed. I didn't want anyone to see me. Ever again.

"I never contacted my old friends. I never saw any of them again. I wanted them to think I was dead. Because, inside, I was dead.

"My aunt and I moved to a new town. I lived with her until she died when I was twenty-five. I kept to myself. I had no friends. I was too ugly to have friends."

She glared at Buddy, who avoided her eyes. He stared past her to the door.

"How — how did you ever find Buddy?" Ashley asked, horrified and fascinated by the story at the same time.

"I paid a visit to the beach house," Maria told her, her eyes on Buddy. "I don't know why. I don't remember. I guess I thought I could ease the pain by walking the beach again, by facing the scene of my nightmare. I crept into the beach house. I was just standing inside, right here in this room, when suddenly I saw Buddy come out of the closet. From thin air. He didn't see me. But I saw him. And then I knew. I knew his secret. I knew the secret of the beach house. I knew how he escaped after killing everyone. The police never figured it out. But I did."

"And you followed Buddy to the future?" Ashley asked, glancing at him as he leaned against the closet door frame, eyeing them both angrily, rubbing his burned shoulder.

"It took me a long time to figure out how," Maria said. "Getting here isn't as easy as going back to 1956. But I was determined to follow Buddy. I was determined. And, finally, I did it. This past spring. But when I came through, I had aged nearly thirty years."

She sighed. "But I didn't care. I really didn't care. I was dead anyway. My life is over. But I came back to make sure your life is over, too, Buddy."

He sneered at her. "You're pitiful," he muttered. "I'm coming out of here now. I'm going home."

She raised the torch, a trail of flame streaking the air. "No, Buddy. I told you, you're never coming out." She pointed the flame at his chest. "Go back to 1956, Buddy. The police are waiting for you back there. Go back and receive the welcome you deserve."

"No way," Buddy scowled, tensing his entire body, preparing to leap out again.

"We still had the electric chair back then," Maria told him, a strange smile playing over her lips. "It's waiting for you. Go back — now. Back is the only direction you can go. Because I'm not letting you out."

"That stupid torch doesn't scare me," Buddy said, his face filled with contempt. "I killed you once, Maria. Do I have to do it again?"

"Do you smell gasoline?" Maria asked, not the least bit impressed by his threat. "Do you, Buddy?"

He didn't reply.

Ashley had smelled it outside. The pungent gasoline aroma was even stronger inside the house.

"I've doused the entire house with it," Maria told him. She lowered the torch, the flame licking at the floor. "Now we're all going to die — for real."

A wave of terror gripped Ashley. She edged toward the window.

Maria meant what she said.

She was going to set the house aflame and kill them all.

She had come through time, sacrificed her youth, sacrificed her entire life for this moment of revenge.

No. No. Please — no, Ashley thought, backing

away, her heart thudding in her chest.

"Don't be stupid. Give me the torch," Buddy said, reaching out a hand for it.

"Back!" Maria ordered. "Back into the closet. Go back, Buddy. They're waiting for you."

"Give me the torch. You're not going to do it," Buddy insisted, his hand outstretched.

Maria hesitated for a brief moment.

Then she cried out, "You want it? Here!"

And she leapt forward and thrust the torch against Buddy's chest. It took only a few seconds for his shirt to flame.

Buddy's eyes bulged in surprise, in horror. He opened his mouth in an angry howl and reared back like a frightened horse.

Maria watched, her face a blank, her eyes cold and hard, as the yellow-orange flames climbed Buddy's chest, danced over his shoulders. She watched him swat wildly, frantically, slapping at his shirt — until his hands and arms were also aflame.

Then, her face still a blank, still dead, Maria lowered the torch to a puddle of gasoline by the doorway.

With a deafening roar, the beach house exploded in flames, killing them all.

31
Ashes

I'm dead. I'm dead.

The words repeated in Ashley's head.

To her amazement, she was flying. Flying through the air.

So this is death, she thought.

Death is flying.

I'm dead and I will fly forever.

But she landed hard on the deck. Outside. The cold, salty air swirling around her. The ocean's roar in her ears.

Outside. I'm outside. On the deck.

And she realized that the explosion had blown her out the window, out of the house, free of the flames that roared louder than the ocean, that reached for her through the gaping hole where the window had been.

Dazed, she was on her feet now. She leapt off the deck, the orange flames howling up to the sky behind her, the entire beach house engulfed, lost behind a wall of fire.

And now she was running across the sand. Running blindly.

Running into Ross's open arms.

Ross?

He *had* followed her.

Ross was there.

Ross, good old Ross.

"Oh, Ross," she managed to say.

She heard the beach house crumple and fall in on itself as the flames triumphed.

Then everything went black, and she died again.

"You're okay," Ross was saying, his worried face hovering over her. "You're okay, Ashley. You just passed out."

A white-jacketed medic loomed beside Ross, a professional smile on his face. "You'll be okay. You've had a real shock."

She raised her head, saw the black-uniformed firemen. They seemed to be everywhere. "The beach house — " she said, choking on the words.

Ross raised a finger to his lips. "Sssh. Don't get up too fast. Take it easy."

"But the beach house — "

"It's gone," he told her. "Nothing left but ashes."

"And Buddy and Maria?" she asked, up on her elbows now, struggling to force away the dizziness.

"Who?"

"Brad and Mary?" she corrected herself.

"Is that who the woman was?" Ross asked, bewildered. "Mary, the maid from Brad's house?"

Ashley nodded. She pulled herself to a sitting position. Someone, she realized, had put a blanket under her to protect her from the wet sand. She took a deep breath. The air was filled with the sweet-sour aroma of burnt wood, as if someone had had a fireplace fire.

"The firemen found a woman's body, completely charred," Ross said. "That's all. No one else."

"No one else?"

Ross shook his head.

Ashley stared at the black ruins of the beach house. A pile of ashes. Firemen were still hosing water on it.

Where was Brad? she wondered.

She had seen him howling in agony, the bright flames crawling over his body.

Did he fall back into the closet? Did he escape back to 1956?

It wouldn't be much of an escape, she knew. Even if he had survived the flames, the electric chair would be waiting for him.

And now that the beach house was gone, there was no way for Brad to come back.

Brad. Buddy. Buddy. Brad.

She sighed, shaking her head. The cold air was beginning to revive her.

"Here come your parents," Ross said, pointing across the beach. "I had the firemen call them from their truck."

Ashley leapt to her feet, eager to see them.

"Ashley! Ashley — what happened?" her mother called.

"Well, it's sort of a long story," Ashley said.

"How do you feel?" Ross asked, turning onto Ocean Drive.

"Great. I feel great," Ashley replied, settling back in the passenger seat. "Especially since summer is just about over."

Ross was taking them for a long ride in his parents' station wagon. Ashley had said earlier that she just wanted to drive and drive and keep going and never look back. "Straight into the future," she had said.

And Ross, glad to be back with her, was eager to oblige.

"It's been such a long, terrible summer," he said thoughtfully, following the curves of the narrow road through the dunes.

"I don't want to talk about it," Ashley replied. "I really don't. Let's just keep going, okay? I just want to sit back and enjoy this night."

"Sounds excellent to me," he said agreeably, reaching over to squeeze her hand.

"And I have one other request," Ashley said, turning to face him.

"What that?"

"Please get this oldies station off the radio!"

Ross obediently changed the station, and they rode on through the rolling, silvery dunes.

About the Author

R.L. STINE is the author of more than two dozen best-selling thrillers and mysteries for young people. Recent titles include *Hit and Run*, *The Girl-friend*, and *The Baby-sitter II*, all published by Scholastic. He is also the author of the *Fear Street* series.

When he isn't writing scary books, he is head writer of the children's TV show, *Eureeka's Castle*, seen on Nickelodeon.

Bob lives in New York City with his wife, Jane, and twelve-year-old son, Matt.

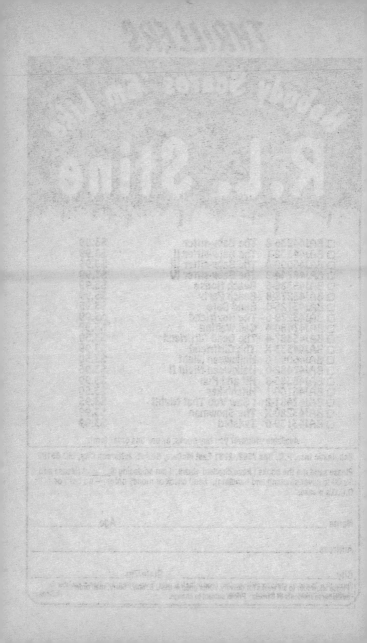

THRILLERS

NIGHTMARE HALL

where college is a scream!

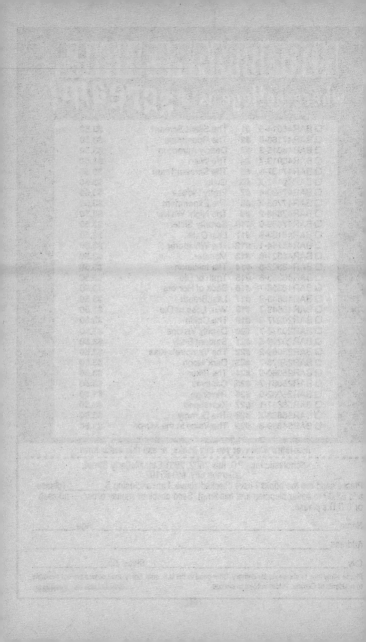